The units are divided into chapters, each of which identifies clear learning outcomes, highlights key vocabulary, lists required resources, points out opportunities for assessing children's learning, and suggests activities for differentiation and extension.

The chapters also include ideas for involving parents, in recognition of the important part they can play. Here, the author suggests ways in which co-operation and two-way communication between the school or nursery and parents can support children's learning.

A special feature of this book is the inclusion of 'Snapshots' which describe everyday events which have been observed in nurseries and reception classrooms during the course of advisory work, teaching practice supervision and school inspection. These 'Snapshots' might help teachers to find opportunities in their own interactions with children to support their learning objectives.

Recommended books

Like a day in the nursery or Reception class, each chapter ends with suggestions for non-fiction texts, stories, rhymes and jingles which can be used to enhance learning, for example:

- *What Do I Look Like?* by Nick Sharratt celebrates the uniqueness of individuals and the different ways in which people show feelings;
- *The Magical Bicycle* by Berlie Doherty and *I Can Build a House* by Shigeo Watanabe applaud achievements which develop self-esteem;
- *The Big Book of Families* by Catherine and Laurence Anholt explores all kinds of families and their relationships;

- *Little Bean's Friend* by John Wallace traces the tentative steps a little girl takes to make friends with the little boy next door;
- *Little Miss Tidy* by Roger Hargreaves is a model of meticulous tidiness – or is she? The children can give their advice;
- *The Tiny Seed* by Eric Carle marvels at the ceaseless miracle of new life.

Many more stories, rhymes and jingles are suggested in the chapters, and are listed in full in a list of resources on page 64. All the recommended books are in print at the time of going to press. Most of them were bought or ordered from high street bookshops. The following booksellers, which accept school requisitions, had excellent selections and were particularly helpful:

Broadbents,
5–7 Market Street,
Southport PR8 1HD.
Tel 01704 532064. Fax 01704 542 009.

Madeleine Lindley,
The Book Centre,
Broadgate,
Chadderton OL9 9XA.
Tel 0161 683 4400. Fax 0161 682 6801.

Pritchards Book Shop,
42 Litherland Road,
Crosby
Liverpool L23 5SF.
Tel 0151 931 1642.

Acknowledgements

The author and publisher thank the staff and children of Greenacre Nursery, Sefton, and Balfour Infants School, Brighton, for their help in carrying out the activities and for allowing themselves and their work to be photographed.

This is me

Intended learning

To develop the children's sense of personal identity and self-worth.

Snapshot

In nursery and reception classes, the development of children's self-esteem is significantly affected by the ways in which the nursery or classroom is organised, and the ways in which the adults interact with the children.

The children had boxes, labelled with their name and decorated with their drawings, in which to keep belongings. They had a place to hang their coats labelled with their name and a small colourful self-portrait.

In this example, using the children's names and giving them their own personal places helped to create a sense of identity.

Key vocabulary

I, me, name, photograph, picture, mirror, face, eyes, ears, hair, nose, mouth

Activities

You will need:

a photograph of each child; unbreakable mirrors of different sizes; a full-length mirror; an easy-to-use automatic-focus camera and film; head-and-shoulders pictures of people from magazines; copies of painted portraits; counters or tokens; paper and card.

Preliminary discussions

● Show a large portrait (face only) photograph of a person the children know or a portrait photograph from a magazine. What can the children see? They could point out the eyes, ears, nose, mouth and hair. Some children might be able to point out other features such as the chin, forehead and eyebrows.

Show them another photograph of a different person, and ask them to look for likenesses and differences between the two people. The children could notice variations in shapes of faces and features, colours of eyes and hair, and lengths and styles of hair.

● Show the children copies of painted portraits and ask them what they can tell about the sitter from things in the picture, such as their interests, pets, home and family. Good examples are *Mr and Mrs Clark and Percy* by David Hockney, *Henry VIII* and *The Ambassadors* by Hans Holbein and *The Reverend Robert Walker Skating on Duddingston Loch* by Henry Raeburn.

● Talk about what the children are able to do. Ask them to complete the sentence 'I can...' with anything they think they do well. They could also describe something they are learning to do. Ask them how they are trying to learn it. The achievement of such targets could be celebrated at a later date by applause from the rest of the class.

After discussion

● Ask the children to look at their face in a mirror and talk about what they see. Ask them about the colour of their eyes, hair and skin. What else do they notice? Then let the children draw self-portraits. One group could try to match the self-portraits drawn by another group with photographs of the same children.

Personal and Social Education

Christine Moorcroft

Illustrations by Alison Dexter
Photographs by Zul Mukhida and Ken Travis

Contents

A & C Black · London

Introduction

The aim of this book is to help teachers to include spiritual, moral, social and cultural education in the curriculum by planning activities which will encourage children to develop:

● self-esteem;
● understanding of different kinds of families;
● the ability to form and maintain relationships;
● respect and sensitivity toward others;
● awareness of the meaning of belonging to a community;
● a sense of responsibility for the environment;
● understanding of right and wrong;
● spiritual awareness;
● independence and responsibility for their own safety and that of others;
● an understanding of health and hygiene and an appropriate sense of responsibility for their own health and hygiene.

Personal and social development has long been regarded as the core of the pre-school curriculum. Its importance is recognised by OFSTED:

Effective provision for spiritual development at the primary and nursery stage depends on a curriculum and approaches to teaching which embody clear values and enable pupils to gain understanding through reflection on their own and other people's values and beliefs, and their environment...

The essence of moral development is to build a framework of values which regulate personal behaviour through principles rather than through punishment or reward. With support, nursery pupils are aware of what is acceptable and unacceptable behaviour...

Social development hinges on an acceptance of group rules and an ability to set oneself in a wider context. For young children... learning how to relate to others and take responsibility for their own actions is an important part of their education...

Cultural development is concerned both with participation in and appreciation of cultural traditions... Aspects of the curriculum such as history, geography, art, music, dance, drama and literature can all make positive contributions...

(Guidance for the Inspection of Nursery and Primary Schools, 1995)

The activities and suggestions in *Personal and Social Education* reflect an understanding that children learn social skills and attitudes from the adults (as well as other children) with whom they come into contact, and that these attitudes and skills are often 'caught' rather than taught, i.e. the ways in which adults and other significant people interact with a child communicate values and expectations.

About this book

The book is divided into several units, each covering different areas for children's personal and social development. The section which focuses on self-esteem (*Myself*) is at the beginning because it underpins a child's attitude to learning. Pre-school children are very dependent upon adults, who help to form their sense of identity. Evidence suggests that children who develop a positive sense of their own worth and their place in society are more easily able to profit from their education than those whose self-image is negative.

Drawing portraits of one another encourages observation and helps children to focus on the many ways in which we are all different.

Next ask the children to look at a partner's face and to draw what they see. Ask them to look at their self-portrait and compare it with the drawing their partner has made of them. How are they alike and how are they different?

● Invite the children to bring to school photographs of themselves. Glue the photographs on to individual cards and help the children to write their first name on their card. These could be laminated and stored, alphabetically, in a box. Each morning and afternoon let the children take their own card and put it into its matching pocket on a large wall display 'caterpillar' to show who is present.

● Ask the children to choose five things they would like to include in a photograph of themselves which would tell other people about them (perhaps a favourite item of clothing, a football, a packet of favourite sweets). To help them to check that they have five things, provide five cards and let them take one for each thing they will have in the portrait.

Help the children to photograph one another with their chosen items. Display the photographs in a book about the class and include photographs of adults who work with the class. From time to time ask the children to find a person in the book. What can they find out about him or her from the photograph?

Assessment

● Can the children describe simple features of people's faces?

● Can they say how people are alike or different?

● Can they find out about people from their portraits?

● Can they say why they chose particular things to include in their photographs?

● Can they identify descriptions which apply to themselves?

● Can they read and write their own names?

Evidence of the children's learning

On arrival each morning and afternoon the children went to put their photographs on their own segments of the caterpillar display. Some of them could find, by looking at the caterpillar, whether their friends had arrived.

The children chose clothes to wear for their portrait and objects to include in it. Some of them explained their choices, for example: 'My football kit, because I'm going to play for Middlesbrough'; 'A sari. I got it in India'; 'A video. It's my best film.'

Differentiating the activities

For children who would benefit from a simpler introductory activity, play a game in which you ask questions about what the children look like. When they recognise a description which applies to themselves they say 'Yes!' and take a counter or token. For example, you might ask, 'Do you have blue eyes?', 'Is your hair brown?', 'Are you wearing a grey skirt?' or 'Have you got short hair?' Stop the game and ask the children to put their counters in lines so that they can see who has the most. He or she is the winner. Help them to count the counters. Eventually the children might be able to take turns to ask the questions themselves.

Extension activities

● The children could take turns to describe someone else in the class. Can the others tell who it is? They might be able to talk about abstract qualities in a person, such as kindness, friendliness, cleverness or shyness. How can they tell if someone is kind, friendly, clever or shy? What does the person do which shows these qualities?

● Make badges which show the children's names and say something about them. Encourage the child to write his or her own name. An adult can transcribe what the child would like the badge to say.

Involving parents

● Ask parents to talk to the children about their personal and family names, and to write them down. Can the children recognise their own first names among a collection of name labels? Parents could help the children to write their names on name tags and inside the covers of books which belong to them.

● Encourage parents to show interest in what their children have to say, by looking at them and giving them their full attention, even if it is only for a few minutes each day.

Using stories and rhymes

What Do I Look Like? by Nick Sharratt (Walker, 1998)

This book invites children to participate from the first page, on which they are asked 'What do you look like?' The little boy in the book shows how he looks when different things happen during the day.

Ask the children to describe the little boy in the story. How does his face change and why? What stays the same? How do their own, their friends', teachers' and parents' faces change, and why? Read with the children the single sentence on each page which begins 'I look like this'. Ask them to look at the picture and predict the ending of the sentence before lifting the flap. They could make their own 'What do I look like?' books.

The Magical Bicycle by Berlie Doherty (Collins Picture Lions, 1996)

The little boy in this story has a new bicycle, but he cannot ride it. He tries again and again, but keeps falling off. Everyone in his family can ride the bicycle, except him. 'There must be a special, secret trick,' he thinks. 'There must be a spell on bikes.' Eventually he learns the magic trick.

Invite the children to describe learning a skill like riding a bicycle or roller-blading. How did they feel when they could not do it? Did they want to give up? Once they could do it, how did they feel and what did they do? Did they rush to show somebody?

I Can Build a House by Shigeo Watanabe (Red Fox, 1982)

The little bear tries to build a house in which he can play. Each one he builds collapses as soon as he gets inside it. He keeps trying and trying, and eventually makes a house from a big box. This time he thinks about it very hard before he begins, and his house is just right!

Talk about things the children have tried very hard to make, and thought they would never get right. How did they feel when things kept going wrong? Did they want to give up? They could talk about giving up and then having another try later. How did they feel when they finally succeeded?

My feelings

Intended learning

To help the children to become aware of the different feelings they have, what might cause them and how they can cope with them; to develop an understanding of how people's feelings can affect others.

Snapshot

Everyday situations in the classroom can be used to help the children to develop an awareness of their own feelings and those of others. They can also help childen learn to cope with 'bad' feelings such as fear, jealousy and anger.

Simon was playing in the sand tray when Natalie snatched the scoop he was using. He responded by angrily throwing sand at her. Once Mrs Parr, the teacher, had made sure there was no sand in Natalie's eyes, she directed both children towards other activities. Later on, Mrs Parr found time to talk to Simon. She asked him how he had felt, and what he thought he should have done when Natalie snatched the scoop. His response was, 'She took it. It was mine.' Mrs Parr agreed with him but pointed out that nobody should throw sand, whatever anyone else does. Later, Mrs Parr asked the class what they felt like doing when they were angry. Some said that they wanted to hit people or throw things. 'What do we have here which is all right to hit or throw?' she asked. Some children said they could throw bean bags or sponge balls outdoors; others said 'play hammering' (using a plastic workbench).

Mrs Parr recognised that Simon needed time to calm down after the incident before he could talk about it. A few days later Gregg knocked over a tower which Simon was building. Simon picked up a block, put it down and went over to Mrs Parr: 'Gregg broke my tower. I didn't throw the bricks. I'm a good boy, aren't I?' He had dealt with his anger in an appropriate way to please Mrs Parr. The next stage would be for him to do so without looking for praise.

Key vocabulary

happy, unhappy, sad, angry, excited, worried, scared, frightened, bored, jealous, proud

Activities

You will need:

painting materials; photographs of people showing feelings (from newspapers, magazines, school resource packs and other sources); dolls, teddy bears and puppets; stories which show people's feelings; information books about feelings; the children's own photographs which show them feeling happy, excited and so on.

Preliminary discussions

● Show the children photographs of people whose feelings are obvious. Ask them how the people feel. How can they tell? You could record and display their responses.

● Ask the children to talk about times when they have felt like the people in the pictures. What did they do when they felt happy, unhappy, excited, worried, scared, bored, proud or jealous? Many children find this easier if they project their feelings on to a character such as a teddy bear. You could suggest, for example: 'Teddy is angry. What has made him angry? He is kicking things and throwing his toys. What could he do instead?'

After discussion

● Provide a collection of pictures of people showing different feelings. A group of children could sort the pictures into sets labelled 'happy', 'sad', 'angry', 'excited' and so on.

● Ask the children to paint pictures of a doll, teddy bear or puppet showing a particular feeling. Help the children to label their pictures to say what he or she is doing, how the character feels and what made him or her feel like that.

● Begin a 'feelings' word-bank, to which the children can contribute when they come across new words for feelings.

● The children could take turns to act out a feeling while the others try to identify it. Talk about what they might do to feel better if they have 'bad' feelings (for example, if they are upset they might cuddle their mother, father, teddy bear or pet). They could draw people experiencing 'bad' feelings, then draw something which might make them feel better.

● Ask the children to bring photographs to school which show them feeling happy, proud and so on. These could be fixed on to a display entitled 'Our good feelings'. They could describe things they have done which have made others happy and create a greetings card to make someone they know feel happy.

The children drew pictures that expressed particular feelings and they made greetings cards to 'make someone happy'. The work was made into a display.

Assessment

● Can the children identify and describe the feelings of people in pictures?

● Do they use appropriate vocabulary when describing feelings?

● Can they say what might make people have particular feelings, such as jealousy, happiness or unhappiness?

● Can they name any actions associated with particular feelings, such as smiling (happy), crying (sad or upset) and frowning (angry)?

● Can they describe some of their own actions which might affect the feelings of others?

● Are they able to classify feelings as 'bad', 'good' or neither?

● Are they able to offer suggestions for coping with 'bad' feelings?

Evidence of the children's learning

On looking at a photograph of a boy smiling broadly, some children thought he had been given a present; others said he was happy, but did not offer any reasons. One said that he was smiling for the photograph!

Most of the children could sort pictures of people and cartoon characters into sets of those showing 'good' and 'bad' feelings, although only a few could name the feelings. They could not agree about the set in which 'excited' people belonged, because some of them thought the people were frightened.

Differentiating the activities

Some children might need extra practice in using words to describe feelings. Show them a teddy bear or doll which is acting in a way which indicates happiness, sadness, and so on, while telling them what the character has done to make him or her feel like this. Let the children decide whether each feeling is 'good', 'bad' or neither. They could help the character to celebrate 'good' feelings and make him or her feel better after having 'bad' feelings.

Extension activities

● Some children might be able to talk about the ways in which they can tell how their parents or teachers feel. How can they tell when their parents or teachers are pleased, angry or disappointed with them?

● They might be able to describe a time when somebody's 'bad' feelings, such as bad temper or jealousy, spoiled things for other people. They could make up a story about such an occasion and suggest what could have been done to make things happier for everyone.

Involving parents

● Encourage parents to talk to the children about the feelings of television characters (including cartoon characters) and what has happened to cause those feelings. They could talk about how they can tell what the characters feel.

● Parents could help the children to find pictures in magazines and comics which show the feelings of people or characters, using the vocabulary associated with feelings. They could cut out the pictures to take into school, where the children could share them with the class.

Using stories and rhymes

I Feel Sad by Brian Moses (Wayland, 1994)

Colourful illustrations show how the little boy in the book feels when he is sad, such as when he feels '…like a flower that needs watering' and '…like a rainbow that has lost its colours.' Pictures and captions tell the reader what the little boy does when he is sad, such as hide in the playhouse and cuddle his teddy. Incidents which have made him sad are shown, and each of them ends with a picture and caption showing what made the little boy feel better.

Ask the children which of the pictures best shows how they feel when they are sad. What do they want to do when they are sad? Have any of the same things made them sad? They could talk about the incidents and say what made them feel better afterwards.

What I Like by Catherine & Laurence Anholt (Walker, 1998)

In this rhyming story a series of children name things they like, such as 'time to play', 'a holiday', 'jumping about' and 'having a shout'; things they do not like, such as getting lost; things they love, such as playing the fool; and then things they hate, like aches, snakes, rats and gnats.

Let the children make their own individual 'What I like' and 'What I don't like' collage pictures. What do they like or dislike about the things in their pictures? Talk about the similarities and differences between their likes and dislikes and those of the children in the book. Can the children name things which they think everyone would like? They could keep a class scrap book of things and events which they all like.

'Sad' from *Waiting for my Shorts to Dry* by Michelle Margorian (Picture Puffins, 1989)

A little girl feels sad, but she cannot explain why. She does not feel like playing or having a story or her tea. She just feels like crying, and having a rest on somebody's knee.

Have the children ever felt sad without knowing why? What did they feel like doing/not doing? What made them feel better? They could draw pictures of the sad little girl and add things to cheer her up.

The people in my home

Intended learning

To develop the children's understanding of 'family' and the names by which the people in their family are known.

Snapshot

By observing the children's role-play in a 'home corner', teachers can discover the children's ideas about families.

Four children were playing in the home corner. 'I'm the dad,' said William. 'I'm the mum,' said Katy. The other two appeared to assume the roles of children (Katy told them to tidy their rooms and go to bed). After about five minutes, William left, saying that he was going to work and would be back for supper. He then joined a group which was engaged in a different activity, and did not return. Another boy went into the home corner where the children greeted him as a new 'dad'. Katy said he could be the 'dad' because she had 'got divorced'.

The children were exploring the roles of different members of a family and the changes which happen within families when parents divorce.

Key vocabulary

mother, father, mummy, daddy, mum, dad, brother, sister, step-, grandfather, grandmother, gran, grandad, grandpa, grandma

Activities

You will need:

photographs of the children's families; photographs of the teacher's and adult helpers' families; pictures of families cut from magazines and newspapers; pictures of individuals from magazines, newspapers and mail order clothing catalogues; wallpaper with a plain reverse side; painting materials; collage materials.

Preliminary discussions

● In a small group, ask the children to show photographs of their families and to name the people in them. What do they call the people in their families? Do other people call them by different names? (For example, what are 'Mum' or 'Dad' called by other people who know them?) Which people have the same names in all their families (mother, father, mum, dad, and so on)?

● Show the children pictures of, and talk about, different kinds of families, for example: one- and two-parent families; families in which there are different numbers of children; families in which all the children have grown up; and families in which there are grandparents and children but no parents. How are these families similar to or different from their own?

● The children could look at photographs of the families of their teachers and other adults. Ask them to identify the person they know in that family. Who do they think the other people might be? Ask them which is the father, which is the mother and so on. How can they tell?

● Talk about the children's surnames or family names. Which name is shared by people in their family?

After discussion

● Help the children to make a concertina book with labelled drawings of their home and the people who live in it. They might want to include pets. The children could find out things about members of their families to include in their books, such as their ages, their jobs, their hobbies, the things they can do well and so on.

● Provide the children with pictures of individuals cut from magazines, mail order clothing catalogues or newspapers, and ask them to make up and name families, using the pictures. Ask them to explain how the people in these families are related: 'Is there a mother? Which one is she? Is there a father? Are there any children? Which ones are brothers/ sisters?' The children could tell the rest of the group or class about the families they have created, and make up stories about them.

Year 6 children helped to make this 'family' collage and helped the younger children to write about the pictures that they had drawn of their families. These were displayed behind the life-size figures.

● The children could contribute to a life-size display of members of a family invented by the class. Help the children to draw round the outlines of people lying full-length on a large piece of paper. Cut out the outlines after the children have painted the faces and clothing or made them with a collage of paper and/or fabric. Fix them on to a background. This could show the invented family's home or it could be made up of children's drawings about their own families.

Assessment

● Can the children name members of their own close family circle?

● Can they name people as mother, father, brother and sister, or the corresponding step-relations, if appropriate?

● Can they describe members of a family they do not know in terms of the mother ('Mum' or 'Mummy'), father ('Dad' or 'Daddy'), brother, sister, and so on?

● Can they name other members of their family, such as grandmothers, grandfathers, aunts, uncles and cousins?

● How many words of 'family' vocabulary do they use?

● When given pictures of people, can they invent families and give the people family names and roles?

Evidence of the children's learning

When making up families using pictures of people from magazines, catalogues and other sources, most of the children created families similar to their own, including their pets. After discussion, some of them could imagine and invent different kinds of families.

Many of the children with pets insisted that their dog or cat was a member of their family because it lived in their home, but they would exclude hamsters, gerbils, fish, guinea pigs and other small animals. One said, in explanation, that the gerbil lived in a cage, but his cat lived in the house. A few said that only people, and not animals, could be in families.

Differentiating the activities

Children who have a very limited vocabulary of 'family' words might benefit from activities in which they identify mothers only, then fathers, brothers, sisters, and so on. Ask them to draw their mother (or other female carer) and help them to label her. Repeat this for their father (or other male carer) and so on.

Extension activities

● Encourage the children to compare their families. Do they have grandparents, cousins or aunts and uncles living in their homes? Do members of their families live in other towns or even in other countries? They could talk about the times when they see them and how they keep in touch.

● The children could make and label pictures of family members who live elsewhere. They could find out the names of the roads and/or towns where they live and include them in their concertina 'family' books.

Involving parents

● Ask parents to teach the children to recite their names and addresses and, if they can, their telephone numbers. They could help the children to identify relatives, such as brother, sister, grandmother, grandfather, and talk about the oldest and youngest family members.

● Encourage parents to talk to the children about family photographs: the people in them, their names, what relation they are to the children and the occasion on which the photograph was taken.

● Parents could show the children photographs taken on family occasions, such as weddings, to help them to identify members of their families whom they do not often see, using their names and terms such as brother, cousin, step-sister and so on.

Using stories and rhymes

The Big Book of Families by Catherine & Laurence Anholt (Walker, 1998)

This book of rhymes opens with a series of illustrated scenes showing things which families do, such as laughing, learning, loving, sharing, shouting and so on. What follows is a tour of everything concerning families of all types, from their homes, names, likes and dislikes, to conversations and silences, delights and worries. Most children will find something with which they can identify.

Show the children the picture in which members of a family stand on one another's shoulders like circus acrobats. Ask them where the oldest and youngest members of the family are placed. With help, they could make pictures which show their own families in a similar way. Ask them who should be at the bottom, who should be next and so on. This will help to develop their idea of generations in a family.

Something Special by Nicola Moon (Orchard, 1995)

This story is about Charlie, whose mother seems to spend all her time feeding, rocking, bathing and dressing the baby, and changing its nappies. Everyone is allowed to take turns to bring something special to school, but when it is Charlie's turn he cannot think of anything. His mother suggests the model boat he made, an African rag doll and a chocolate rabbit, but none of them seems special in comparison with Lu Mei's dragon kite or Raju's Indian sweets. Then he has an idea – he asks his mother to take his baby sister to school!

Ask the children to talk about people in their families and what makes them special. They could bring photographs of a family member to school and, perhaps, special things connected with him or her, such as a toy, a certificate, equipment used in their hobbies or a special thing they wear, such as a uniform.

Bye Bye Baby by Janet & Allan Ahlberg (Mammoth, 1991)

A baby lives all alone. He feeds and bathes himself and even changes his own nappy, but he has no mummy. He decides one night that he needs a mummy – so off he goes to look for one. He asks people and animals he meets if they will be his mummy, but cannot find one. After falling and bumping his head, he begins to cry, 'I want my mummy.' Just then a woman comes by pushing an empty pram. The baby tells her that he wants a mummy. She tells him she is a mummy with no baby, and they live happily ever after.

Ask the children about the things the baby has to do for himself. What can they do for themselves, and what do their parents still need to do for them? Ask them, too, what the baby in the story does which might have been dangerous (he went off with a stranger) and which they must not do.

Helping one another

Intended learning

To develop an appreciation of the ways in which members of a family can help and support one another; to develop an understanding of some of the conflicts within families; to consider how to deal with such situations.

Snapshot

Play in a 'home corner' can be structured to enable the children to enact the everyday jobs which have to be done in a home.

In the home corner, the children were deciding who was going to do each of the jobs they had decided needed to be done (preparing dinner, washing up, cleaning the carpet, cleaning the windows and feeding the pets). They all wanted to feed the pets and clean the carpet (because the toy vacuum cleaner sounded impressively like a real one, and it worked!), but none wanted to wash up. Maya said that it wasn't fair if Simon had 'all the nice jobs'; Rosie just did as she was told and said little. Mrs Carter asked Rosie what they should do to make the division of tools fair. 'Take turns,' she replied. Mrs Carter said this was a good idea.

Rosie had to be encouraged to join in the role-play. The adult helper drew her into the discussion and the activity, and helped to raise her status in the eyes of the other children.

Key vocabulary

share, help, sorry, play, work

Activities

You will need:

a corner of the classroom set up as a 'home'; glove puppets representing adults and children; dolls or model people (including adults and children of different races); art straws; a stapler; stiff paper or thin card.

Preliminary discussions

● Invite the children to talk about the things they do with their families, such as shopping, reading, eating, watching television, playing, washing up, tidying the home and so on.

● Talk about the things the children's parents (and perhaps grandparents) do for them. What do the children do for their parents?

● Can the children suggest anything people might do which spoils things for others with whom they live? Examples might include making a lot of noise, doing things which take up a lot of space, switching channels on television while others are watching it and so on.

● Talk about the meaning of 'thinking of others' and 'being considerate'. What can the children do at home which shows that they are thinking of others and being considerate?

● Ask the children what they think is good and naughty behaviour at home. They could talk about the things children do which make their parents cross. Can they explain why parents tell their children off? What can parents and children do to stop this happening so often?

After discussion

● Provide a 'family' of dolls to which the children can assign roles, such as mother, step-mother, father, step-father, grandfather, grandmother, baby, brother or sister. Each day the children could contribute information about this invented family which an adult could transcribe and display. They could make up family events such as mealtimes, birthdays, weddings, days out and holidays.

Invent incidents of conflict in the doll 'family' and ask the children what might happen next. For example, you might arrange two dolls to look as if they are fighting, or to look like two adults arguing. You might set one doll alone, looking sad. Ask the children what the dolls are doing and why they are fighting/quarrelling/sad. The children could suggest what might be done in each situation.

● Invite groups of children to enact the roles of members of a family in the home corner. Talk to them about the activities they choose to do in their roles. For example, whose job is it in their pretend family to clean the home, tidy up, make the meals, do repairs, cut the grass, wash the car and so on? Could these jobs be done by anyone else in the family?

● Let the children draw or paint pictures of activities in which members of their family help one another with shopping, tidying up at home, playing games, going for walks, reading stories with brothers or sisters and so on.

The children drew pictures to show how members of their families help one another. With adult assistance, they word-processed their accounts.

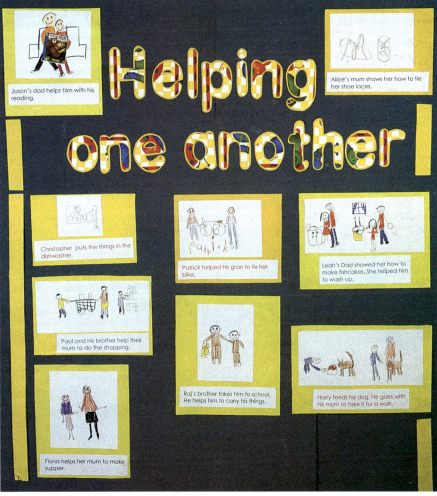

Assessment

● In a role-play situation, do the children contribute to conversations and activities?

● Can they talk about things which members of a family do together?

● Do they offer ideas for resolving family conflicts in the class's invented family?

● Can they name some of the things which are shared by members of their family?

● Can they describe any problems which arise when people share things?

● Can they suggest reasons why their parents or carers tell them off and ways to prevent this happening too often?

Evidence of the children's learning

The children often played with the dolls, sometimes alone (holding imaginary conversations between members of the 'family'), and sometimes with two or three other children, when they would tell one another what the dolls were doing. The latter often became a role-play situation, with the children taking the parts of members of the 'family'. Sometimes conflicts arose (for example, when the 'mother' told the children it was time for bed and they did not want to go). The children usually negotiated with one another to resolve these conflicts.

Differentiating the activities

● Some children might benefit from the opportunity to talk about pictures of families engaged in shared activities.

● Ask the children what they like doing best with people in their families. They could bring to school photographs of themselves doing the activity, or the objects associated with it, such as a football, a game or an item of clothing. Encourage them to talk about the object to the rest of the group and to tell them how they use it with someone in their family.

Extension activities

● Some children might be able to enact family situations using puppets, to which they could allocate roles. The characters could have 'conversations'.

● With practice the children could present puppet plays about their invented families. They could make the puppets using art straws and paper, fixed together with tape.

Involving parents

● Encourage parents to talk to the children about what they do when they are at home, shopping or enjoying leisure time. They could talk about an activity the children enjoy doing with them or with other relatives.

● Parents could let the children bring to school an object associated with an activity they do together, such as a dish-washing mop, a safe gardening item, a special item of clothing, a shopping bag and till receipt, a dog's lead or a can of cat food. In school the children could show the object and ask the others to guess what they have been doing with their families.

Using stories and rhymes

Poems from *Waiting for my Shorts to Dry* by Michelle Margorian (Picture Puffins, 1989):
'Granny's Armchair'

This is about a special place where a little girl sits with her grandmother – a very big, very old arm-chair which has room for both of them as well as a collection of dolls and teddy bears. The little girl's mother wants her to get rid of the chair because it is too big and too old, but Granny insists, 'Oh no, I can't do that.'

Ask the children what the little girl, her grand-mother and her mother think about the arm-chair. Why does the mother want to get rid of it? Why do the little girl and her grandmother want to keep it? Do the children think the little girl's mother will get rid of the chair? Why not? Talk about the special places which people in the children's families have. For whom are they special? Who might want to change them? Why? The children could draw or paint pic-tures of these people in their special places and say what makes them special.

'Goodbye'
A little girl has been told off by her parents. She tells them that she is going to run away, that they cannot stop her, that they will be sorry when she has gone and will wish they had been nicer to her. At the end of the poem she opens the front door, but changes her mind because 'I expect you'll be lonely without me', adding that even though they are mean, she has decided to stay.

Have the children ever threatened to run away after being told off? What did they do and say? Did they pack a bag? The children could describe their thoughts as they were about to go. Did they change their minds? Why? They could describe what they said to their parents. Teachers and other adults could tell the children about times when they were told off by their parents, about any times when they wanted to run away and about how they changed their minds.

The Mice Who Lived in a Shoe by Rodney Peppé (Picture Puffins, 1981)

A family of mice lives in an old shoe which is too hot in the summer, too cold in the winter and lets in the rain and wind. They get together and decide to re-build their house. Each mouse offers to do one of the jobs. Before they begin, they draw plans for the new house and Father collects their ideas from which to make the final plan. Then the building begins. Each mouse co-operates in a great team effort, with friends and relatives joining in.

Ask the children how they think the mice felt when they had finished building their beauti-ful, new house. What might make them feel proud? (They had *all* helped, and so the house really did belong to all of them.) The children could describe jobs they have done with mem-bers of their families. What do they like and dislike about sharing work?

Making friends

Intended learning

To develop an ability to empathise with others; to learn to form and maintain friendships.

Snapshot

In addition to planned activities, everyday situations can be used by teachers to encourage children to develop relationships.

The children had set up a 'garage' in the classroom. Ms Roy saw May watching the others, looking as if she wanted to join in. Ms Roy told May that her car needed an oil check; could she help her to do it? They checked the 'car' and Ms Roy asked some of the other children what sort of work they had been doing on cars that day. They had replaced tyres, fixed lights and filled cars with petrol. May joined in, saying that she had been checking the oil.

Ms Roy recognised that May wanted to play with the others, but was shy. She was able to encourage May without drawing special attention to her, and to help her to become part of the group.

Key vocabulary

friend, look after, talk, play, kind

Activities

You will need:

stories about making friends; card; a display board; pictures of individuals of different ages and races; pictures of friends together.

Preliminary discussions

● Talk about everyday events which show how people can be good friends to one another. Examples might include: looking after a child who has been hurt; inviting another child to play; listening while someone is talking; sharing things (see pages 24–27 which focus on this); and comforting someone who is upset.

● Ask the children what they would do if their friend was crying. What would they say? How would they help him or her to feel better? What would they do if their friend had some good news? How would they share it? What would they do if their friend had a new bicycle or new clothes?

The children could talk about times when others have been good friends to them and they to others.

● Ask the children to name a friend and talk about some of the things they do together. Teachers and other adults who work with the children need to ensure that no child feels that he or she has been left out. Children who do not make friends easily in the school or nursery might have friends at home about whom they can be encouraged to talk.

● Ask the children if they have ever fallen out with a friend. Why? How did they make friends again? Did one of them say sorry?

● Do any of the children count animals as friends? They could talk about their animal friends and what makes them a good friend. Is the animal always pleased to see them when they wake up in the morning or come home from school? How does it show that it is pleased to see them?

After discussion

● Make a display entitled 'Friends' which shows pictures of people of different ages and races with their friends. The pictures could include photographs from home, pictures from magazines or newspapers and paintings or drawings contributed by the children.

Encourage the children to look at the collage and talk about the people in it. How can they tell they are friends? What are they doing? An adult could transcribe their responses and incorporate them into the display.

● Show the class pictures of other children of different races and ages. Ask the children whom they would choose for a friend and why.

● Ask the children to talk about how they would try to make friends with someone. What sort of things might stop people from making friends? The children could make a tape recording of their ideas or draw a picture of someone trying to make friends and someone behaving in a way which stops others wanting to be their friend.

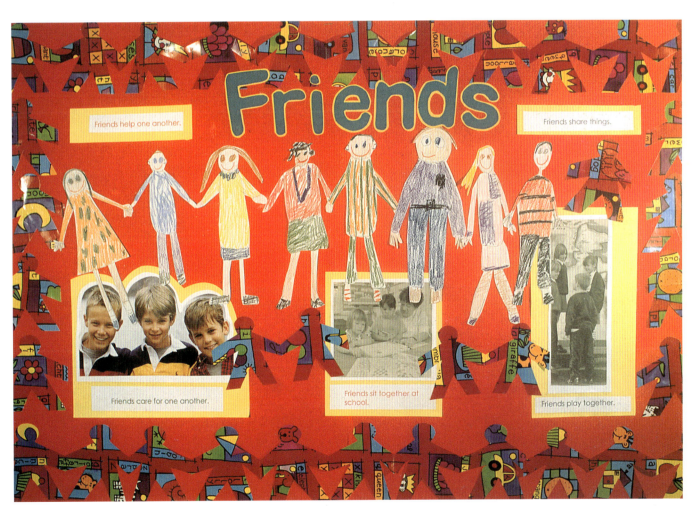

An adult helped the children to word-process their descriptions of what friends do together, and added these to the 'Friends' display.

Assessment

● Do the children offer ideas about how they can show friendship?

● Do they readily play with other children?

● Are they confident in joining other children playing, or do they need encouragement?

● Do they encourage others who are shy to join their group?

● During play, do they engage in conversation and show friendship towards other children?

Evidence of the children's learning

When the children were shown pictures of people and asked whom they would choose as a friend, they tended to choose those of the same race, gender and age as themselves. The teacher asked if girls and boys could be friends. One girl said, 'Thomas is my friend. But he's not my boyfriend.' Other girls said that they had friends who were boys. Only one boy thought that boys could have friends who were girls. When asked why they would not choose certain people as friends, they often answered, 'I don't like him/her,' but could not say why. When asked why they liked one person better than another, their answers became more focused: 'She's got a nicer face', 'He looks happy', 'He's too old'. Some children said that, to make friends, they would say 'hello', offer them a sweet, invite them to their party or ask if they can sit by them. After discussion, they added more suggestions: smiling, asking their name and asking them about their favourite games and television programmes.

Differentiating the activities

Some children might benefit from talking about friendships which they have heard stories about, or which they have seen on television. The children could name the friends of the characters. What do the friends do? How do they show they are friends? They could make pictures and label them (for example, 'Laa-Laa and her friend Po').

Extension activities

● Some children might be able to draw and label pictures of the friends they have made in different places, for example: at home; in school or nursery; at clubs or other organisations; at the homes of their parents' friends; and at places to which they go with their parents, such as leisure centres and shops.

● Ask the children to make up 'instructions for making friends'. The instructions should focus on positive things as well as what people should *not* do if they want to make friends. An adult could transcribe or word-process them.

Involving parents

Parents could ask the children to talk about their friends and what it is they like about them. They could also talk to the children about their own friends, saying why they like them and what they like to do with them. They could talk about a time when they have fallen out with a friend, what caused it, how they felt and how they made up again.

Using stories and rhymes

Little Bean's Friend by John Wallace (Collins Picture Lions, 1996)

Little Bean plays alone with her slide, her toy house, her sand pit, a hose pipe and her tricycle, and splashes in her paddling pool. She plays with her dog, and then she meets the little boy next door. She runs off to find her father, who asks her why she does not go and say 'Hello' to the little boy. Before long she is playing with her things again but, this time, with her new friend Paul.

Ask the children which they think was more fun for Little Bean: playing alone or playing with Paul? What difference did it make to have a friend with whom to play? The children could draw pictures of things they like doing with friends. Ask the children how Little Bean made friends with her next-door neighbour. What would the children do if they wanted to make friends with someone?

Handa's Surprise by Eileen Brown (Walker, 1994)

Handa plans a surprise for her friend Akeyo who lives in the next village. She selects seven fruits and puts them in a basket, which she puts on her head before setting off on foot. On the way, Handa thinks about the pleasure the gift will bring her friend and does not see the animals which steal the fruit. Eventually the basket is empty, but Handa passes a tree which a goat butts, sending dozens of tangerines cascading into the basket. Handa, as well as Akeyo, is surprised when she arrives at the village!

Talk about the care with which Handa chooses the fruits for her friend. Have the children chosen a present for a friend? Did they make it or buy it? Ask them to think of a surprise they could make for someone of whom they are fond. They could think about the things which interest the person, about their favourite foods and colours and about their hobbies.

The Bad-Tempered Ladybird by Eric Carle (Picture Puffins, 1977)

The bad-tempered ladybird rejects all offers of friendship from other animals. It is mean, rude and aggressive. It thinks it is better than everyone else, but eventually learns to be friendly.

Ask the children to compare the behaviour of the two ladybirds at the beginning of the story. What does the friendly one do? What does the unfriendly one do and how has it changed by the end of the story? Groups of children could enact friendly and unfriendly behaviour while others watch and decide whether they are being friendly or unfriendly.

Sharing

Intended learning

To develop a willingness to share; to learn to take turns to use things; to learn to take turns to speak and listen during conversations.

Snapshot

Many everyday activities provide opportunities to develop the children's interpersonal skills, including sharing and taking turns.

The reception class had three tricycles which were in great demand during outdoor play. Jack, Polly and Sean always managed to get them when they wanted them. The reactions of the other children varied: some complained to the teacher; others told Jack, Polly and Sean that it wasn't fair, and asked for a turn to ride a tricycle; one cried; but many of them just accepted the situation.

The teacher found an opportunity to talk to the class about the tricycles. Was it fair that the quickest or biggest children should always have a tricycle? What could be done to make things fairer? Several ideas came from the children. The one they agreed on was to have cards which they would give the teacher when they wanted to ride a tricycle. Children whose cards were with the teacher could have another turn only if the others did not want to. The children made decorated name cards. One of them even drew a picture of a tricycle to put on the box. Soon the children were managing the tricycle-sharing without help from the teacher. Instead of giving her their cards, they found a shoe-box with a lid in which they made a slot for sliding the cards. The box was kept firmly closed with an elastic band.

The teacher helped the children themselves to resolve a conflict. Because they had come up with the solution, they felt ownership of it, and they kept to it. They developed interpersonal skills by working as a team and, at the same time, they were using some very sophisticated problem-solving skills. This opportunity would have been denied to them if the teacher had imposed a solution.

Key vocabulary

share, take turns, listen, talk, speak

Activities

You will need:

a small bag made from a piece of fabric tied with a ribbon; board games.

Preliminary discussions

● What do the children share with their friends or with others in their group or class? Perhaps they sometimes have to wait a long time for their turn to use equipment. What happens when children will not share?

● Ask the children what they did at playtime. If several children speak at once, ask the others if they can hear what is being said. Why not? The children could be asked to find a solution. How can they make sure that everyone has a turn to speak?

● Talk to the children about everyday problems they have in sharing things and taking turns, and ask them to think of solutions. Make a note of their ideas and read them back at the end of the discussion. Which do they think would work the best? Help them to refine the chosen idea to make it feasible.

After discussion

● Play games which require taking turns. Include board games in which the progression of taking turns is clockwise, and games in which the children themselves decide whose turn is next, such as *Lucy Locket*. In this game the children sit on the floor in a circle, and the teacher chooses one child to skip round the outside carrying something to represent a pocket, such as a small cloth bag, while the others sing:

> *Lucy Locket lost her pocket,*
> *Kitty Fisher found it.*
> *There was not a penny in it,*
> *But a ribbon round it.*
> *Please, please drop it, drop it, drop it…*

…until the child chooses to drop the 'pocket' in the lap of another, whose turn it then is to skip round the circle.

● Ask the children to organise fair ways in which to take turns to use equipment.

● Make a display about taking turns. The children could draw pictures of the things they do in the nursery or school which involve taking turns. They could also include the times when they have to take turns outside school, such as when they queue in a shop or they wait to see a doctor. An adult can label the children's drawings and transcribe what they say about them.

Playing games such as *Lucy Locket* helped the children understand the importance of taking turns.

Assessment

● Can the children describe what happens when people do not take turns?

● Can they offer reasons why they should take turns?

● Do they recognise ways in which adults take turns in the home and other places?

● Can they name some of these?

● Can they talk about the ways in which shops, banks and post offices make sure that people wait their turn to be served?

● Do they take turns in conversations and in using equipment?

● Can they think up ways to ensure the fair taking of turns in the classroom or nursery?

Evidence of the children's learning

During their play, the children talked about taking turns. Sometimes, during games, they would forget to wait their turn, only to be reminded by the others. Some of them would take responsibility for ensuring that everyone in their group had his or her turn to join in a game or to use equipment.

In role-play areas such as the class 'shop', the children showed an awareness of the need to wait their turn. They made use of systems they had seen in everyday life, particularly the use of numbered tickets, which also developed their mathematical skills.

Differentiating the activities

Let the children play a game in pairs which involves building a tower, taking turns to add a block until the tower collapses. The winner is the last to add a block which does not make the tower collapse. Ask the children who should go first. If both children want to go first, how can they decide fairly? (They could toss a coin, throw a die or draw lots.) As they take their turn to add a block, encourage them to use the words 'my turn' and 'your turn'.

Extension activities

● Some children might be able to think up ways in which to decide who has the first turn in games or equipment-sharing. They could collaborate to make a booklet, which the rest of the class could use for reference, called 'Who goes first?' They could glue their drawings and writing into it.

● The children could find out about the ways in which adults ensure fair play in games and other situations, for example: tossing a coin; drawing lots; choosing a number or, as at supermarket delicatessen counters, taking a ticket and then waiting for their ticket number to be indicated. The children could introduce this system into a class 'shop'. Some of them might be able to number the tickets to ensure that everyone is served in the correct order.

Involving parents

● Parents could show the children the ways in which they have to take turns, for example: queuing in shops; stopping at traffic lights; letting other cars pass them on narrow roads;

waiting for buses or trains; waiting at zebra crossings (as pedestrians or drivers); and waiting for other people in the family to finish using things such as a salt cellar or telephone.

● Ask parents to help their children to find out about the systems used in banks, post offices and shops to help the cashiers serve people in turn, for example, using numbered tickets or a recorded voice to direct people to vacant counters.

Using stories and rhymes

This is Our House by Michael Rosen (Walker, 1996)

George plays house in an enormous cardboard box. The other children want to play, too, but George refuses to let them in. 'This house is mine and no one else is coming in!' he insists. They try to reason with him, but to no avail: he guards it fiercely, managing to keep out seven other would-be inhabitants and a dog. Eventually he has to leave the 'house' to go to the toilet! The others seize their chance and leap in. When George returns they won't let him in, but by now the house is so crowded that it falls apart.

Help the children to make a house like the one in the story. They could take turns to enact the story using some of the words from the book and/or some of their own. (The children could substitute their own names and the names of their friends for those in the story.) The 'house' could be used as a prop. The children could practise their 'plays', then perform them for the rest of the class.

Giving by Shirley Hughes (Walker, 1995)

A little girl describes the things she gives and is given: presents, hugs, kisses, pictures she has painted, a slice of apple, a cross look, a smile and so on.

Talk about the things the children give, including 'things' like presents and sweets, and 'not things' like hugs, looks and kisses. Ask them what they have given today. They could make a collage to show all the things they like giving. What do people give them which they like?

The people in my school

Intended learning

To develop the children's understanding of what it means to belong to a community and of the roles key people play in the school community; to develop awareness of how people can show respect for one another through politeness.

Snapshot

Children can learn how to treat others with politeness from their interactions with other people and their observations of adults who work in the school. Sometimes, however, the example provided by teachers and other adults has to be emphasised and reinforced.

The teachers and other adult helpers in one nursery consistently addressed the children and one another politely but the children showed few signs of noticing it. They decided to bring politeness to the attention of the class. For a week, they recorded any instances they noticed of children behaving politely towards one another or adults. During the same day they would recount the incidents to the class and ask the children concerned to demonstrate what they had done while the others watched and listened. Mrs Moore also asked the children if they had spotted anything polite.

Mrs Moore and the other staff realised that the example they were setting reinforced children's learning but that, for many of the children in their care, this was their first experience of politeness and they first had to be taught it.

Key vocabulary

teacher, secretary, cleaner, cook, caretaker, gardener, please, thank you, excuse me, I'm sorry

Activities

You will need:

a simple automatic-focus camera; painting, drawing, writing and cutting materials.

Preliminary discussions

● Ask the children to name people who work in the school. What are their jobs? These might include the school secretary, cleaner, caretaker, lunch-time assistants and voluntary helpers. Ask the children what the school would be like without one of these people.

● Can the children think of ways to help these people to do their work? For example, helping the cleaner might mean putting chairs on the tables at the end of the day and making sure they have not left equipment on the floor. Ask them how they could help (or do help) other people in the school.

● Demonstrate different ways of asking the children to do something (with and without the word 'please'; in different tones of voice). Which ways do they think are polite? Talk about some of the polite words people use when they ask for things, respond to questions or try to pass somebody. Introduce the word 'community', explaining that the school and the children's families are all communities, i.e. groups of people who live or work together.

A cleaner was invited to talk to the children about her work.

After discussion

● Arrange for people who work in the school to spend a short time talking to the class. The children could be helped to interview the guest speakers about their jobs. They might ask about the different tasks they have to do, what they like best about their work, what they like least and what made them choose that work.

Before an interview, ask the children how they can make their visitors feel welcome and comfortable. What can they say and do and how can they thank them afterwards?

The people interviewed could show the children some of the things which they use in their work and talk about how they use them. The children could photograph, draw or paint pictures of some of these things.

● A booklet could be compiled about people who work in the school, using the children's drawings, paintings, writing and photography. Alternatively, a 'welcome' display could be made in the school foyer which also includes pictures of the children themselves.

● Help the children to make giant 'thank you' cards for the people they have interviewed. Help them to create a special card for each person, for example: a card for the cook could be made in the shape of a cooking pot containing the children's individual messages.

The children helped to make this 'thank you' card for the gardener.

Assessment

● Do the children use the word 'please' when asking for things?

● Do they thank people (including other children) for any help they are given?

● Do they say 'excuse me' when they want to pass people?

● Can they identify people who work in the school?

● Can they name important work which these people do?

Evidence of the children's learning

When sharing equipment, children asked one another to pass items such as felt-tipped pens, using the word 'please'. Some of them then complained if this did not produce the desired results! 'I said "please" but Amy wouldn't give me the scissors,' said one girl. Another said, 'It feels nice when they say "thank you".' One response was, 'I like Liam saying "excuse me"; he doesn't push me.'

Some of the children were able to match photographs of people who work in the school to items of equipment they use and to say how they use it. They could enact the roles of people such as the secretary and cleaner.

Differentiating the activities

● Ask the children to name things for which they have thanked people, or things for which they forgot to thank someone.

● They could paint pictures of times when they should thank people, for example: when their friends' parents have invited them to their homes; when someone has given them a present; when someone has allowed them to do something; or when someone has said something nice to them. They could include the words 'thank you' in their pictures. Display their pictures together under the heading 'Our polite community'.

Extension activities

Some children might be able to recognise other communities to which they belong (such as activity clubs or a church, mosque, synagogue, temple or other place of worship). Ask them about the people who have special jobs in these communities. What do they do, what equipment do they use and what do they have to know about? The children could tell the rest of the group or class about the work of a person from this other community.

Involving parents

● Parents could talk to the children about the people who worked in their own school communities and discuss the similarities and differences between their roles and those of people who work in the children's school.

● Let parents know that there will be an emphasis on good manners in the classroom and nursery, mentioning key words which will be used: 'please', 'thank you' and 'excuse me'.

● Parents could enter information in a notebook, shared with the teacher and child, about the times when the child has shown good manners at home.

Using stories and rhymes

The Oxford Nursery Rhyme Book by Iona & Peter Opie (Oxford University Press, 1997)

A chapter of this book provides a selection of rhymes about 'Good Manners', some of whose words can be changed to make them easier for the children to understand, for example:

> Manners in the dining room,
> Manners in the hall.
> If you don't behave yourself,
> You'll have nothing at all.

and

> Hearts, like doors, will open with ease
> To very, very little keys,
> And don't forget that two of these
> Are 'thank you' and 'if you please'.

The House that Jack Built (traditional) (Ladybird, 1987)

This well-known story, told in verses, describes the community which inhabits Jack's house and its surroundings: Jack himself, the rat which stole the malt, the cat which killed the rat, the dog which worried the cat, the cow which tossed the dog, the maiden who milked the cow, the man who kissed the maiden, the priest who married them, the cock which crowed to wake them each morning and the farmer who sowed the corn.

Ask the children which people were kind to one another or did useful things and which ones were unkind or unhelpful. What could have made the community in Jack's house a happier one?

Goodnight Owl by Pat Hutchins (Picture Puffins, 1972)

Owl tries to sleep, but the other animals who live in and around the tree make a lot of noise in the day-time: the bees buzz, the squirrel cracks nuts, the crows croak, the woodpecker pecks, the star-lings chitter, the jays scream, the cuckoo calls, the robin peeps, the sparrows chirp, and the doves coo. All this noise keeps Owl awake. As night falls the animals become tired. Soon they are all fast asleep – then Owl screeches and wakes them all up!

Ask the children to name the animals which belonged to the community in the tree. Did they show consideration to one another? How could they have been more considerate? The children could think about ways in which they them-selves are or are not considerate to others in their class community. Can they think of a time when they were trying to work quietly but found it difficult because of the actions of others? They could make a display to show considerate ways in which to behave in the classroom.

Taking care of things

Intended learning

To develop in the children a sense of responsibility for the care of equipment and materials in the classroom or nursery.

Snapshot

The care which teachers and other adults take of the classroom and its equipment will provide an example for the children. The children themselves can also be encouraged to help to create a pleasant working environment.

In one reception classroom, a display board (which the children could reach) was set aside on which the children could display work of their choice. They could choose from a collection of coloured backing paper and had been shown how to use it to make their work look attractive. Sometimes they selected things for display with the help of their teacher, parents or adult helper. The reason for their choice was sometimes transcribed or word-processed by an adult and sometimes written by the children, and was displayed. The date was written on everything, so that when space was needed for something new, the oldest displayed item could be removed. To assist the children in replacing equipment after use, the teacher labelled containers for things like pencils, scissors, crayons, blocks and shells with a picture and the name of the things they held.

By making the display board the property of the children, the teacher encouraged the children to feel ownership of the classroom.

Key vocabulary

care, look after, clean, tidy, comfortable, attractive, pretty

Activities

You will need:

painting and drawing materials; photographs (taken by the teacher) of the same areas of the classroom when they were neglected and when they were cared for.

Preliminary discussions

● Ask the children what they like about their classroom. Encourage them to use all their senses and introduce words which mean 'nice'. What looks attractive, smells sweet, feels comfortable? Ask them about their favourite parts of the classroom. What do they like about them? Are there any parts they do not like? How could these parts be improved?

● Talk about the ways in which the children can take care of the classroom. What can they do to keep it attractive? How can they make sure things are not damaged?

After discussion

● Help the children to carry out an audit of the classroom, noting the good points and the things which need to be changed. They could plan the changes and put into practice any of their plans which are feasible.

● Let children choose something in the classroom for which they would like to be responsible (a box of equipment, a plant, a shelf of books, a display). They could look after it on a rota basis with other children.

These children chose to be responsible for keeping the book displays tidy.

● Take photographs of areas of the classroom when they look their best and when they have been neglected. The children could sort the pictures into two sets: 'Pleasant' and 'Unpleasant'. Ask them how each place became unpleasant and how it can be made pleasant again.

● Select items in the classroom which have to be looked after and ask the children to think up messages which the objects might want to give, such as 'Wash the paint off me' (a paintbrush), 'Put me back on the shelf' (a book) and 'Sharpen me when I'm blunt' (a pencil).

Assessment

● Can the children identify what they like and dislike about their classroom?

● Can they say what actions can keep the classroom pleasant and what actions stop this?

● Are they willing to take responsibility for the care of part of their classroom? How well do they do this?

● Do they put equipment away after use and clean it when appropriate?

● How well do they care for their own belongings?

Evidence of the children's learning

The children thought of ways in which they could make the school 'smell nice'. Some thought of bringing in plants and other things with pleasant smells. One brought to school perfume tester strips which her mother had collected in a department store (these were fastened to a display board in the classroom); another brought a bunch of lavender.

Many children began to show greater care for their own and others' property. It became more common for children to return pencils, wax crayons, etc. to the places where they were kept.

Differentiating the activities

● The children could examine some of their own belongings, such as shoes, pencils and lunchboxes, and decide how well they have looked after them. Their answers could be recorded on a chart. What can they do to look after their things better?

Extension activities

● The children could contribute ideas to a board game which depicts ways in which they care for or neglect the classroom environment and property belonging to other people.

● Some children could talk about things which they have borrowed from others. How well did they look after these things? Have they ever had their own belongings mistreated by others? How did they feel about this?

Involving parents

● Parents could help the children to choose an item at home which has not been well looked after (a bush in the garden, a book, a cushion), and then plan what they will do to make up for the neglect. Can it be mended? Does it need to be washed? Who will do it and how?

● The children might be allowed to take responsibility for the care of something at home if they do not do so already, such as a pet, a plant, or their bedroom. They could draw pictures to show how they care for it.

Using stories and rhymes

This is the Bear by Sarah Hayes (Walker, 1986)

The dog pushes the teddy bear into a bin. The rubbish is taken to the tip. 'Stop!' cries the little boy who owns the bear; 'Stop!' cries the bear from inside the black bin-liner, but nobody hears. The little boy and his dog catch a bus to the tip, where he asks the man in charge if he will find his bear. 'You must be joking,' says the man, but he sees the tears in the little boy's eyes and helps him to search through the rubbish. He even drives him home afterwards.

Ask the children to predict and then find out what happens to the bear at the end of the story. Have they ever lost something precious because they have not looked after it properly? How did they feel? Could they put things right? Do they have any possessions of which they take special care? How do they keep them safe?

'Mary, Mary' (Traditional) in *The Oxford Nursery Rhyme Book*, by Iona & Peter Opie (Oxford University Press, 1997)

In this well-known rhyme, Mary has a garden to look after, filled with 'silver bells and cockle shells and pretty maids all in a row'.

Ask the children to imagine the garden. Is it tidy or untidy? How can they tell? (They should be able to work out that it is tidy from the words 'all in a row'.) A large collage could be made of the garden, to which the children could contribute flowers and other things which they have drawn, painted or made from coloured paper. Alternatively, the children could make miniature models of the garden in old saucers. The saucers could be filled with sand or soil from a clean area of the school grounds into which the children can push small flowers, leaves, shells and stones.

Little Miss Tidy by Roger Hargreaves (World International, 1990)

Little Miss Tidy has lots of boxes into which she puts things when she tidies up. But she often forgets where she has put things such as her hairbrush, purse and telephone.

Read the story up to Little Miss Tidy's birthday. Ask the children what is wrong with her tidying. What could she do to improve it? Read the rest of the story and ask the children if they can think of a better present than a notebook for Little Miss Tidy. (She could use labels on which to write the contents of each box.) The children could devise methods for storing things in the classroom so that they are easy to find.

Rules

Intended learning

To appreciate the need for rules in the class and school and for the children to help to formulate these rules.

Snapshot

In every school or nursery, teachers convey their expectations about the ways in which children should behave.

Ms Stone kept a note of the 'good' and 'bad' behaviour she observed in the nursery, and found a weekly opportunity to talk to the children about some of her observations. She described the behaviour and asked the children whether they thought it was good or bad, and why. The children began to talk about their own behaviour in terms of how it affected other people and the safety of themselves and others. For example, Meera said that they should not run in the classroom because they might hurt someone ('And we could break things,' added Ross).

Ms Stone helped the children to learn to recognise right and wrong (mainly in connection with the comfort, happiness and safety of themselves and others) in contexts which were familiar to them. They were able to use this learning in their everyday activities. She reinforced the kind of behaviour she wanted from the children by publicly praising them for it and she discouraged anti-social behaviour by making sure that the children knew it was unacceptable. They were not 'named' during the discussion sessions, but they knew Ms Stone was referring to their own behaviour.

Key vocabulary

considerate, safe, happy, unhappy, good, bad, right, wrong, naughty

Activities

You will need:

pictures of children behaving 'badly' and behaving 'well'; writing, drawing and painting materials; model classroom equipment and model people; indoor board and card games with simple rules; a ball, and perhaps a bat, for outdoor games.

Preliminary discussions

● Ask the children if their mothers, fathers or other carers ever tell them they are good. What do they do to deserve being called 'good'? List some of this behaviour and ask the children what makes it good or right. Is the same behaviour good in school? Why?

Then ask them about things for which they are told off at home, and for which they are told off at school. What makes this behaviour bad or wrong? Is the same behaviour bad at home and at school?

● Ask the children to imagine a classroom in which there are no rules, where everyone does just as he or she likes. What would they do in such a classroom? Would they be happy if they could do as they liked? Would it be a good place to be? Why not? What might happen? Ask them why they think there should be rules.

After discussion

● Play games which have a few simple rules (these could be outdoor games or indoor games). Once the children have played the game, ask them to describe some of its rules. What are players allowed to do, and what are they not allowed to do? Why? They could draw pictures to illustrate the rules and to show what might happen if players did not follow them.

● Ask the children to think up some rules for their own classroom which an adult could transcribe or which the children could tape-record. Ask them why they think each rule is needed. During a plenary session they could tell the rest of the class the rules they have thought up. Ask them to give examples of behaviour which would show that someone is obeying each of these rules.

Let the children contribute to illustrated posters displaying the rules which they have agreed for their class and which could be read with them at regular intervals. This is an opportunity to praise or reward groups or individuals for obeying the rules.

The 'Rules' poster could have a space next to each rule where a 'happy face' could be fixed at the end of a morning or afternoon when everyone has obeyed that rule. You could use a 'sad face' if some of the children have disobeyed it.

The children were encouraged to think about the idea of rules by playing simple board games.

Assessment

● Can the children identify examples of good and bad behaviour?

● Can they describe one or two rules of a familiar game?

● Can they say why rules are needed in the classroom?

● Can they suggest fair penalties for disobeying rules?

● Can they name any rules which adults have to obey? Can they say what happens if they do not obey the rules?

Evidence of the children's learning

The children's first suggestions for rules began with 'Don't': 'Don't run in the classroom', 'Don't hit people', 'Don't snatch things'. When they were asked to think of things they *should* do, they began with very general suggestions such as 'Be good' and 'Be quiet'. When asked for examples of good behaviour, suggestions included 'Talk quietly', 'Let someone else go first' and 'Tidy the class shop'. Some of the children suggested very logical punishments for disobeying rules, such as 'Tidy up every day' (for leaving the 'making table' untidy) and 'Be quiet for all of playtime' (for shouting in class).

One child said that a rule of 'Snap' was taking turns. Another said that the first person to say 'Snap' won all the cards in the pile, but 'only if they're right'. Another said 'You're out if you have no cards left,' adding, 'you're not allowed to throw the cards when you're out.'

Differentiating the activities

● Provide a collection of model people and a model classroom in which the children can enter into make-believe situations. Ask them to make some of the 'children' in the 'class' be good and some bad. What do they think the teacher should do about the good and the bad behaviour?

● Give the children some pictorial or verbal examples of behaviour and ask them to decide whether each one is 'good' or 'bad' and why.

Extension activities

Ask the children what should happen if they disobey one of their class rules. Should there be punishments? What kind of punishments do the children think should be given? They could draw and write about their ideas which could be glued on to cards and kept in a box or plastic wallet for future reference.

Involving parents

● Parents could talk to the children about rules they think there should be at home. The children could be helped to make a daily diary in which just one rule is written (for example, 'Put your toys away at bed-time' or 'Be nice to your little brother'). Parents could draw a happy face next to the dates on which the children have obeyed the rule.

● Parents could talk about the rules which they themselves have to obey (and the penalties for not doing so), such as speed limits, cleaning up after their dog fouls a pavement, putting litter in bins and arriving at their work on time.

Using stories and rhymes

'Ding Dong Bell' and 'Kindness' (Traditional) in *The Oxford Nursery Rhyme Book* by Iona & Peter Opie (Oxford University Press, 1997)

As the first rhyme tells us, Little Johnny Green threw the cat down the well, and Little Tommy Stout pulled her out.

Let the children learn the rhyme and repeat it to enjoy its rhythm and rhyme, but ask them to think about what happens in it. Whose behaviour was good and whose was bad? They could talk about right and wrong ways in which to treat animals. Help them to find out about a local or national organisation which cares for animals. A visitor from the organisation could talk to the children about his or her work, and the children could help to raise funds for the organisation.

The second rhyme is about caring for a cat:

> *I love little Pussy,*
> *Her coat is so warm,*
> *And if I don't hurt her*
> *She'll do me no harm.*
> *So I'll not pull her tail,*
> *Nor drive her away,*
> *But Pussy and I*
> *Very gently will play.*
> *She shall sit by my side,*
> *And I'll give her some food;*
> *And Pussy will love me*
> *Because I am good.*

Ask the children to identify the ways in which the child is kind to the cat, and the unkind actions which he or she does *not* do.

The children could make a display about kindness to animals which includes their drawings and paintings of animals and instructions for caring for them. (Whenever possible, provide real animals or photographs of them for the children to draw or paint.)

I Don't Care by Brian Moses & Mike Gordon (Wayland, 1997)

This book explains what 'respect' means. It shows the ways in which children show disrespect and respect for others in different situations, it introduces the need for rules in communities such as schools and shows some of the ways in which the children's words can show respect for the feelings of others.

Spare copies of the book could be cut up and the pictures glued on to card with the words in speech bubbles deleted. The children could tell the story of what is happening in each picture and suggest some words with which to complete the empty speech bubbles.

Nature

Intended learning

To develop the children's sense of wonder about nature; to develop their curiosity about, and respect for, the natural world.

Snapshot

The ways in which teachers and other adults treat, and talk about, the natural world influences the children's attitudes towards nature.

One January Ms Carter arranged a bunch of what looked like dead twigs in a jug of water. Each day, the children were asked to look at them and at the bush in the school grounds from which they had been cut. 'Something special will happen to them,' said Ms Carter. Sure enough, buds began to appear on the twigs within a week, while the bush outside remained bare. Before long the children noticed that something green looked as if it was about to burst out of some of the buds, while other buds looked more yellow – and then it happened: the yellow buds blossomed into tiny star-shaped flowers and the green ones into delicate leaves. The children watched and talked about this each day, and each day they looked at the bush outside, which was still bare. They learned the name of their special bush – forsythia. Two years later some of those children still bring forsythia twigs indoors in January and watch for the buds, leaves and flowers to appear.

Ms Carter's own sense of the magic of nature helped her to enthuse the children. She built up their feelings of expectation and enjoyment of nature in a way they are likely to remember for a long time.

Key vocabulary

care, living, non-living, nature, lovely, delicate, enormous, clever

Activities

You will need:

photographs of beautiful or impressive things in nature, for example: a spider's web coated with dew, a waterfall, a volcano and a snail's shell; some real examples, such as a flower, a gourd or an intricately-patterned stone; painting and drawing materials; coloured paper; one small box per child; scissors.

Preliminary discussions

● Give the children a natural object, chosen for its beauty, to examine. What can they see and feel? The children could talk about patterns, colours, textures and warmth or coolness. Does it have a smell? Introduce words such as delicate, rounded, smooth, rough, sharp, spiky and twisted. Ask the children whether the thing they are looking at is dead or alive. Has it ever been alive or been part of a living thing?

● Show the children photographs of natural things of beauty and invite them to talk about what it would be like to be part of the picture? The children could think about what they might see, hear, smell and feel. Would it be warm or cool? Would it be wet or dry? Would they want to be quiet and still or to run about and make a lot of noise if they were in the picture?

The children contributed to a picture of the park. As they observed changes there, they made changes to the display. They replaced the green leaves on the tree with russet and gold leaves, and they put 'ice' on the pond.

After discussion

● Give the children a small box to take on a walk in the school grounds or in a nearby park. Ask them to find beautiful things (but not animals) to put in the box. Back in the classroom, make a display of the finds.

● Stimulate the children's interest with an 'amazing things in nature' display. This might include the pattern of a snowflake or a snail's shell, a picture of a weaver bird's or a red ants' nest, the patterns on flowers which help bees to find their way to the pollen, or pictures of animals like frogs and salmon, which find their way back to the place in which they were spawned.

● Make a display showing a park or a part of the school grounds which changes with the seasons. Shoots of different plants could appear in the ground, and could 'flower' at appropriate times of the year. Different animals (including birds and insects) could appear on the picture at the appropriate times.

The children drew pictures and wrote about Autumn.

Assessment

● Do the children notice the seasonal changes in their immediate surroundings, such as the changing colours of leaves?

● Can they suggest ways to change the 'seasons' display?

● Are they aware that the cycle of seasonal changes is repeated every year?

● Can they identify something natural which they think is beautiful?

● Can they recognise things which are living?

● Do they show curiosity about the natural world by making observations and asking questions based on their observations?

Evidence of the children's learning

Some of the children were fascinated to notice how long roses stayed in flower. Each day they would say, 'It's *still* got flowers'. It was December before they decided to remove the flowers from the roses in the changing display. Several children remembered, without prompting, to cut out a golden, orange or brown leaf with which to replace a green leaf on one of the trees in the display. It was the children who decided when it was time to start taking leaves off the trees. One or two of them had noticed that the leaves on some trees stayed green and that the leaves of some trees did not fall off. One little boy asked the teacher how the trees knew it was autumn, and another said to him that they could feel it getting colder.

Differentiating the activities

The teacher or other adult could tell the chidren about (or show them pictures or a video of) something which has amazed him or her in nature – perhaps the features of a landscape, plants or animals. They could describe their fascination with it and encourage the children to ask questions about it.

Extension activities

● The children could sort pictures or objects into two sets: 'Made by people' and 'Natural'. Invite them to add things of their own choice to each set. Ask the the children to choose the most beautiful thing in each set and say what they think makes it beautiful.

● Help the children to make a survey of beautiful things in the school grounds. How can they help them to stay beautiful? The children could name things which cause damage, such as litter, vandalism and graffiti.Then they could suggest ways to prevent damage, for example, by the provision of litter bins and information posters which ask people to look after the grounds. The children's ideas could be recorded on a chart.

Involving parents

Encourage parents to talk to the children about the changes they see happening in nature, such as the appearance of buds, leaves, flowers, fruits and seeds on plants, and the presence of different animals at different times of the year.

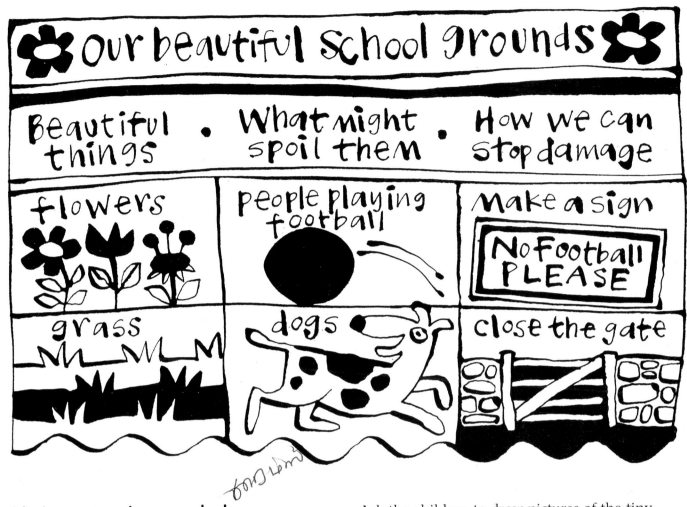

Our beautiful school grounds		
Beautiful things	What might spoil them	How we can stop damage
flowers	people playing football	make a sign — No Football PLEASE
grass	dogs	close the gate

Using stories and rhymes

The Tiny Seed by Eric Carle (Picture Puffins, 1997)

The book begins in the autumn when a tiny seed is blown by the wind across mountain-tops and ice, an ocean and a desert. In the winter, the tiny seed escapes being eaten by a mouse and a bird. It stays on the ground, covered by snow, through the winter. In the spring it grows a shoot. By the summer, it has grown into a huge plant with a big, brightly-coloured flower. The birds and butterflies visit it, then its petals begin to fall. Before long there are none left – but it has lots of seeds.

Ask the children to draw pictures of the tiny seed's life story on separate pieces of paper, which they can then put in order. If they make a straight line, ask them what happens at the end of the story and ask them to look again at what happened at the beginning. They should see that the story sequence can be arranged in a circle to show the life cycle of a plant. Let them take a seed from a quick-growing plant like a tomato, plant it and watch the plant through its life cycle, until it produces more tomatoes and seeds.

Celebrating

Intended learning

To develop an appreciation of the feeling of celebration, the events which people celebrate and the ways in which they celebrate them.

Snapshot

Children can gain an appreciation of the meaning of celebration through the school's own celebrations of important events and achievements.

Mr Walker kept a note of his reception children's special achievements, such as learning to write their addresses, counting to five, ten, fifteen or higher, and learning to tie their shoe-laces. Each Friday a small ceremony was held to congratulate those children. Mr Walker ensured that everyone was congratulated for something during each half-term.

In this first snapshot, Mr Walker helped the children to take part in the shared celebration of a child's achievement.

Mrs Strong began each morning and afternoon session in the nursery with ten minutes of 'circle time', during which the children could take a turn to tell the others about something which interested them. She encouraged them to talk about anything they were celebrating at home and to bring in special things they used in their celebrations. Some of these sessions were later developed into activities, such as tasting some of the foods eaten at Eid-ul-Fitr, making clay Divali lamps and baking hot-cross buns. The knowledge and expertise of parents were often valuable during these activities.

In this second snapshot, Mrs Strong helped the children to develop an understanding of one another's cultural backgrounds and gave them opportunities to experience some of the various ways in which people celebrate significant events.

Key vocabulary

celebrate, food, clap, dance, sing, birthday, present, gift, card

Activities

You will need:

different kinds of bicycles and tricycles; pictures of bicycles and tricycles; scrap fabrics; ribbon; coloured paper; writing and drawing materials.

Preliminary discussions

● Talk about something which many of the children celebrate, such as birthdays (note that many Muslims and Jehovah's Witnesses do not celebrate birthdays). What do they do on their birthdays? Ask them about special foods they eat, games they play, songs they sing, dances they do and about birthday parties or outings. Ask them when their next birthday will be. Do they know how often they have a birthday and how often they celebrate festivals like Christmas or Divali?

● Take a teddy bear into the classroom and tell the children that it is going to be his birthday soon. Ask them to contribute ideas for a special birthday tea-party.

After discussion

● A party 'with a difference' could be planned by telling the children that Teddy likes riding his bike and he wants a 'bicycle' party. Show the children different kinds of bicycles and tricycles (real ones as far as possible, with pictures of others). Include a grocer's delivery bike, complete with its basket, and ask them how this might be useful (it could be used for carrying a picnic).

With their parents' co-operation the children could bring their own bikes to school and decorate them with coloured streamers and ribbons. (Ensure that none is long enough to become tangled in the wheels.)

The party could include a bike ride around the school grounds and an outdoor picnic, carried in bicycle baskets and saddle bags.
Help the children to make special foods for the picnic, such as teddy-bear-shaped sandwiches and biscuits. (Teddy-bear-shaped cutters are available from specialist cake-making suppliers.)

Help the children to make party outfits for dolls and teddy bears from scrap material and ribbons. They could make paper hats for themselves and for the dolls and teddy bears.

The children held a special birthday tea-party for Teddy and friends.

Assessment

● Can the children name events which they celebrate with their families?

● Do they know how often they celebrate these events?

● Can they talk about the ways in which they celebrate their birthdays and other events?

● Can they name special foods they eat during the celebrations?

● Can they name and talk about special clothes they wear for celebrations?

● Can they describe how they feel during the days before a celebration?

Evidence of the children's learning

In the role-play area, one girl prepared a teddy bear for his birthday party. She dressed him and told him that he had to keep himself clean and tidy for the party. Every now and again she turned to him and said, 'No, it's not yet – not until six o'clock.' Meanwhile she was setting a table for the party, complete with a Plasticine birthday cake with five candles.

One boy brought to school a rakhi (a bracelet made from fabrics, ribbons and tinsel) which his sister had given to him at Rakshabandhan, the Hindu festival which celebrates the bonds between brothers and sisters. He said that on that special day he and his sister gave one another presents and made up for the times they had argued. He said, 'It feels nice. Everyone is happy.'

Differentiating the activities

● Provide a role-play area in which the children can enact birthday parties. Include clothes in which to dress up, materials for making paper hats, plastic plates, dishes, cups and cutlery, writing and gift-wrapping materials and Plasticine.

● On the birthday of a child in the class, the children could sing 'Happy Birthday to You'.

Extension activities

● Some children might be able to make invitations to Teddy's birthday party. Ask them what the people coming to the party will need to know (the date, starting and finishing times, where it is to be held and, for a bicycle party, that they will need to bring a bicycle). Ask them what else needs to be on the invitation (a reply slip to let Teddy know whether or not they can come).

● They might be able to make a time-line of birthday cards, if possible from their previous birthdays, which has a card for each year of their lives.

Involving parents

● Parents could involve the children in planning celebrations at home, such as family birthdays and community events like Divali, Christmas, Eid-ul-Fitr, Holi and Purim.

● They could help the children to put together a collection of items to show to the class when they tell them about their celebrations. Some parents might even be able to visit the nursery or school to show the class some of their celebration activities, such as marking mendhi patterns on their hands for Divali or making Hamantaschen (sweet pastries) for Purim.

Using stories and rhymes

Kipper's Birthday by Mick Inkpen
(Hodder & Stoughton, 1993)

A dog called Kipper prepares for his birthday party. He paints invitations, bakes a cake and rushes out to get balloons which he has forgotten. Finally, everything is ready and Kipper waits for his guests to arrive – but nobody comes. While he is waiting, he begins to eat bits of the birthday cake until, five hours later, it has all gone. Kipper falls asleep. Then the next day there is a knock on his front door. There are all his guests, carrying birthday presents!

Can the children work out what went wrong? (Kipper's invitations bore the words 'Please come to my party tomorrow at 12 o'clock.') Despite the problem, Kipper and his friends enjoyed the party. Ask the children to explain which present was the most useful (the cake) and why (Kipper had eaten the first one).

When Frank Was Four by Alison Lester
(Little Ark Books, Allen & Unwin, 1997)

When Nicky was one she tipped spaghetti on her head and Rosie first said 'horse'; when Tessa was two she stopped wearing nappies and Celeste began to sleep all night; when Ernie was three he gave away his dummy and Nicky got stuck in a tree... In this book, a group of children's memorable events are described up to the age of seven.

Ask the children to find out from their parents about one event from each year of their lives. Let them make books entitled 'When I Was One, Two, Three, Four and Five'. Each week in school could be devoted to memories from one year of the children's lives about which they could talk to the others. Make a time-line to which each child can contribute a picture of something from a year of his or her life.

Getting Ready for Eid by Roderick Hunt
(Oxford University Press, 1994)

Adam and Yasmin and their family are getting ready for Eid-ul-Fitr at the end of the month of Ramadan. Yasmin fasts during Ramadan, but Adam does not because he is too young. They are both excited about the party they are going to have with their relatives, some of whom have made a special trip from Pakistan. The children enjoy the preparation: new clothes, mendhi patterns on the women's and girls' hands, the buying of gifts and making of special foods.

Talk about the times when many people in a family meet for a special occasion. How do the children feel while they are waiting for their relatives to arrive or when they themselves are going to visit them? The children could draw pictures of family gatherings. Ask them to find out where members of their families live, and for what occasions they all get together. How do the children and their parents prepare for special occasions? Invite the children to bring to school clothes they have worn for a special occasion and greetings cards they have received. Label and display their cards.

Keeping safe

Intended learning

To develop an awareness of potential dangers in the children's immediate surroundings; to help children to begin to take appropriate responsibility for their own safety.

Snapshot

The children can be encouraged to help to keep the nursery or classroom safe for themselves and others.

Megan had been drawing. She got up from her seat and knocked over a pot of crayons. Some fell on the floor, but she left them there. At the same time, William left some large wooden beads on the carpet. Ms Lake asked them to pick up the things. Later, during a whole-class discussion, Ms Lake told the children she had seen crayons and beads on the floor. What might happen if they had not been picked up? At first, the children said that the crayons and beads might get lost or broken. 'But what might happen to someone who did not see them and trod on them?' she asked. The children realised that accidents could be caused if they left things on the floor. They talked about other things which could cause similar accidents, such as sand and water.

Mrs Lake encouraged the children to take some responsibility for their own safety and that of others by taking care of the equipment they used.

Key vocabulary

sharp, poisonous, electrical, electricity, plug, socket, wire, hot, fire, medicine

Activities

You will need:

pictures of objects, some of which are safe for children to handle and others which are potentially dangerous (electrical appliances, poisonous plants, bottles, sharp objects); photographs of places, such as a shopping centre, a nursery playground, a public park, a library, a busy main road, a car park, a deserted lane, a garden, a tool-shed, a building site and a railway line; materials for making a display.

Preliminary discussions

● Ask the children to name places in which they feel safe. Are there any places in which most of the children feel safe? List these. Ask the children why so many of them feel safe in these places. Are there places in which they feel safe only if they have someone to look after them, such as an unfamiliar shop, a busy road or a crowded football ground? List those which are named by most of the children. Why do they feel safer if they have someone with them in these places?

● Can the children name places in which it is safe to play? Where must they not play? Add any unsafe places which the children do not mention, such as building sites, railways, garages, cupboards, disused refrigerators, roads and places where there is glass or other litter. What might happen if they play in these places?

After discussion

● Invite the children to sort a collection of photographs of places into two sets: 'Safe for play' and 'Not safe for play'. Transcribe the children's explanations for their sorting. The photographs and the children's explanations can be displayed in a class 'Safety' book.

● Show the children pictures of everyday objects and ask them which they themselves can use and which are for grown-ups only. Display the sets on a chart.

● Let the children check the school for safety. They could look for things like covers on electrical sockets, tidy equipment and safe (rounded) coat hooks. Encourage them to look for potential dangers, such as untidy or broken equipment, or water on the floor.

● Make a 'Safety in the sun' display. Talk about safe things to do on a sunny day and ask the children to choose one of these to draw. The pictures should include playing or sitting in the shade, wearing a sun hat and using sun cream. Empty tubes of sun cream, sun hats and a parasol could be stapled to the display.

Helping to set up a 'Safety in the sun' display.

Assessment

● Do the children pick up equipment which has been dropped on the floor?

● Can they name everyday things which they must not touch?

● Can they explain why they must not touch them?

● Do they recognise their own achievement in using everyday things, such as table knives, glasses and televisions, safely?

● Do they recognise places which are safe or unsafe to play in, and say why some places are not safe for play?

Evidence of the children's learning

Two children's investigations in the water-tray left more water on the floor and on themselves than in the tray itself. They covered the wet floor with newspapers, informed the teacher how good they were, and waited to be praised.

The children proudly described 'grown-up' things they could do safely. One said, 'I used to bite glasses. I had to have a plastic one. I don't bite them now and I don't drop them.' Others used the class television and video to demonstrate their skills in selecting channels and video programmes. One said that his mum told him to take his time because if he pressed lots of buttons at once it might break. They agreed that they should not touch the plug or socket. Some said that there were safety gates in their homes to stop a younger child going upstairs, and that they were allowed to open the gates but had be sure that they closed them again.

Differentiating the activities

Provide a collection of model people and model school furniture (commercially available sets are suitable) to enable the children to create a classroom and to invent things which happen in it. They could make up an accident in the model classroom and explain how the accident happened. Ask them to make the 'classroom' safe so that there will be no more accidents. They could tell an adult what they have done to make the classroom safe.

Extension activities

Let the children make displays of pictures (cut from brochures and magazines) of 'sharp things', 'poisonous things', 'electrical things' and 'hot things'. Each display could include a face with a speech bubble, saying 'Don't touch'. Ask them to explain to the rest of the class why they must not touch each item.

Involving parents

● Parents could point out to the children anything in their home which could be dangerous if not used properly, for example: electrical sockets, an oven, hot-plates or gas burners, heaters, kettles, knives, tools, plastic bags, cleaning materials and medicines. They could show the children how they themselves use the items in a safe way, while explaining that they are not safe for children to use.

● Parents could talk about things which the children can now use but which are dangerous for babies to use, such as table knives, forks and drinking glasses. Some parents be able to photograph their children using these 'grown-up' things safely.

● Warning notices could be read and explained to the children. These could be notices on electricity sub-stations and pylons, and near railways, level crossings, ponds, canals, concealed entrances and driveways.

Using stories and rhymes

Bedtime Bears by Susanna Gretz
(Hippo/Scholastic,1990)

Four bears play hide-and-seek. One looks for some-where to hide. A plant-pot is too small, the dustbin is too smelly, the bath is too cold and the book-case is too uncomfortable – but the bed is just right. They play other games, such as follow-my-leader and pillow fights. One of them has an accident – he tries to carry too many things upstairs and trips on a long, trailing blanket, spilling a mug of hot cocoa.

Ask the children what makes some places dangerous? Where can they hide safely at home, in the school grounds or in the park?

Ask the children to name the things the bear in the story tried to carry upstairs. They could take turns to add something to the list. How could he have taken all these things upstairs safely? (He could have made more than one journey; he could have asked an adult for help with the bed-cover and the hot drink.) Which things should he not have tried to carry? Why not? Talk about the need to ask adults for help with big, heavy or hot things.

'Round and Round the Garden' (Traditional) in *The Oxford Nursery Book* by Ian Beck (Oxford University Press, 1995):

> *Round and round the garden*
> *Like a teddy bear;*
> *One step, two step,*
> *Tickle you under there!*

Allow the children to make up their own end-ings which say why some places in the garden are not safe for play, for example:

> Round and round the garden
> Like a teddy bear.
> No, it's dirty;
> You can't play there!

and

> Round and round the garden,
> Like a teddy bear.
> No, there's a car;
> You can't play there!

The food I eat

Intended learning

For the children to appreciate the need to eat a variety of different foods and to develop a willingness to try 'new' foods.

Snapshot

The children can be introduced to unfamiliar foods during 'snack time'; this is also an opportunity to talk about different *types* of foods.

The snack offered to the children during the mid-morning or mid-afternoon break at the nursery was usually a familiar food such as a sweet or savoury biscuit, a slice of apple or (if it was someone's birthday) a piece of cake. From time to time Mr Seddon would offer the children a less familiar snack, such as a slice of mango or star-fruit, a piece of bara brith, some hummus or a piece of halva. Mr Seddon would ask the children what kind of food it was: whether it was a fruit, a vegetable, a cake, a biscuit and so on.

Sometimes Ms Patel would ask her reception class about their lunch, and she would tell them about hers. If somebody had brought a food which others had never tasted, she would sometimes bring that food to school for them all to sample. They talked about likes and dislikes. If children said, 'I don't like...' Ms Patel would ask if they had ever tasted it: did they really dislike it or did they just *think* they would dislike it?

Neither teacher in the Snapshots imposed on the children his or her own idea of 'healthy' foods. They both recognised, and conveyed to the children, the importance of a varied diet, and avoided branding any food as 'good' or 'bad'.

Key vocabulary

fruit, **vegetable**, **sweet**, **savoury**, **strong**, **grow**, **energy**, **healthy**

Activities

You will need:

selections of foods of a similar type, such as fruits, biscuits, breads, cakes, vegetables or cheeses (include some which most of the children have not tasted); plates; ingredients for a lunch box.

Preliminary discussions

● Do the children know why we need food and drinks? Talk about energy and ask the children what they think it means. The children might have formed their own ideas about energy from information in advertisements, especially for products like glucose drinks, cereals and chocolate bars. They could give examples of the ways in which they use energy for moving around and for keeping warm.

● Talk about food and growth. Tell the children that parts of the foods they eat become part of their bodies and that different foods are good for building skin, bones, teeth, nails, muscles and hair.

After discussion

● Provide four ready-packed lunch boxes for the children to examine: one containing only fruit, one containing only sandwiches, one filled with sweets and another filled with drinks. Is any one of these a healthy lunch? Why not? Let the children make up four 'healthy' lunch boxes using the foods provided. Ask them to explain why the new lunch boxes are healthier than the old ones.

The children drew and described the contents of their lunch boxes.

● Ask the children to draw and cut out pictures of lunch boxes, filled with food to make 'healthy' lunches.

● Help the children to prepare a lunch box which is both fun and healthy (check with their parents for health problems such as allergies).

● Make 'Swiss roll' sandwiches. Spread one side of a slice of bread with margarine and then a filling, such as fish- or meat-paste, cream cheese or hard-boiled egg mashed with mayonnaise. Roll the sandwiches Swiss-roll style and wrap them in foil or cling-film.

● Make tangy orange jellies by cutting an orange in half and scooping out the flesh. (You could put the flesh in a blender and, later, mix it with the jelly filling.) Make the jelly by using less boiling water than suggested on the packet, and topping it up with the juice (and blended flesh) from the orange. Once this has been added, the mixture will be cool enough for the children to stir. They can pour the jelly mixture into the orange halves and leave them to set.

● Provide food packages and pictures of foods which the children can put into sets of 'fruit', 'vegetables', 'biscuits', 'cakes', 'bread' and so on.

Assessment

● Can the children talk about why they need food?

● Can they use the word 'energy' in relation to their actions?

● Do they try 'new' foods?

● Can they make up a 'healthy' lunch box (one which contains three or four different kinds of foods)?

● Can they allocate a picture of a familiar food to a set labelled 'fruit', 'cheese', etc.?

Evidence of the children's learning

The children showed a developing awareness of balanced meals. When making up a 'healthy lunch box', one boy told his friend that he would like the box which just had sweets in it, but added, 'We can't have that – it's not healthy.' 'You can have *some* sweets,' his friend said. They both selected a sandwich, a piece of fruit, a drink and one of the sweets.

In a 'restaurant' role-play, three children sat at a table and chose a meal from the menu. The 'waiter' told them they could not have three puddings: 'You have to have something from here' (pointing to the main courses), 'something from here' (indicating the sweets) 'and a drink.' One of the 'diners' noticed the Starters section and said, 'My Mum says we can have something from here.'

Differentiating the activities

● Have separate tasting sessions for different kinds of food, such as fruits, cheeses, vegetables and biscuits, ensuring that there are samples of foods which the children might not have tasted before. The children could draw or paint the cut out pictures to make collages of one kind of food, which can be labelled.

● After each tasting session, ask the children what new foods they tasted. Which ones did they like? Which did they not like? They could draw and cut out their favourite food from each tasting session, label it and glue it on to a picture of a table. On their picture they could write 'I like these new foods'.

Extension activities

● Draw a block graph on to which children can glue pictures of their favourite fruits.

our.favourite.fruits

fruit:	1	2	3	4	5	6
🍎apple	●	●	●	●	●	
🍌banana	●	●	●	●	●	●
🍒cherry	●	●	●	●		
🍇grape	●	●	●	●		
✳kiwi	●					
🍈melon	●	●				
🍊orange	●	●	●	●	●	
🍐pear	●	●	●			
🍑peach	●					

number of people

● Set up a 'restaurant' in which the children can prepare and serve meals and create menus. Provide real menus from restaurants, recipes from cookery books and magazines, cutlery, crockery, napkins, a tablecloth, salt and pepper pots. The contents of the restaurant could be changed from time to time to maintain the children's interest. Sometimes they could be given a task such as 'making a meal' for somebody who cannot eat nuts, a vegetarian or somebody who does not eat pig meat.

Involving parents

● Ask the children's parents to help them to collect menus, food packets and pictures of food from shop leaflets and magazines.

● Parents could help the children to read the signs in supermarkets which show the types of food in each aisle. They could also read with the children large menus displayed in fast-food restaurants and help the children to copy the names of foods they like.

Using stories and rhymes

Avocado Baby by John Burningham (Red Fox, 1994)

This story is about Mr and Mrs Hargraves and their two children, who are all very weak. Mr and Mrs Hargraves hope that their new baby will be strong; but no, the baby, too, turns out to be weak. He dislikes any food offered – except avocado pear. The avocado diet endows the baby with superhuman strength: he rescues his big brother and sister from two bullies, and throws a burglar out of the house.

Talk about the sorts of foods babies eat. The children should have noticed that babies have no teeth, and so they cannot chew. If possible, ask a mother to bring her baby into the class for a feed and to talk about baby-feeding. Show the children a picture of a two-month-old baby and pictures of foods, such as chips, a carrot, milk, canned baby food, steak, curry, a packet of baby cereal – and an avocado. Ask them what the baby could or could not eat.

Show the children an avocado. Do they know what is inside it? Cut it open and point out the skin, flesh and stone. Give each child a small piece to taste. Do they like it? Tell them it is a fruit, and ask them to name other fruits. They could examine a collection of fruits, including an avocado, and sort them according to the texture of their skins (smooth, rough or bumpy), colour or size. Cut open the fruits and ask the children to notice which have tiny seeds, which have pips and which have stones.

The Baked Bean Queen by Rose Impey & Sue Porter (Picture Puffins, 1986)

A little girl tells the story of her sister who will eat nothing but baked beans. She describes how her mother hides other foods such as sausages in her sister's baked beans – but she always finds them and refuses to eat them with a loud 'NO!'

Are there any foods the children eat more often than others? Are there any foods they will not eat? Why is it not a good idea to eat baked beans (or any kind of food) and nothing else? The children could collect pictures of foods which help build healthy bones, teeth and muscles, keep their skin healthy and give them energy to move around and keep warm.

Keeping clean

Intended learning

To help the children to develop a responsibility for their own personal hygiene.

Snapshots

Everyday life in the nursery or classroom offers many opportunities for developing hygienic habits. Teachers and other adults can set examples for the children to follow, such as tying back long hair and washing their hands before handling food. Health visits also offer a useful starting point for discussion and learning activities.

After a visit by the school health visitor to check for head-lice, the children wanted to know more about the pests. They were enthralled by the pictures she showed them, and with the idea that these insects could live on their hair. They spent a lot of time inspecting one another's hair and showed extreme disappointment at not finding any creatures. The health visitor returned with a video which showed head-lice laying eggs, hatching and jumping from one child's hair to another's. The children watched with rapt attention. The health visitor explained that head-lice like clean hair just as much as dirty hair, and explained to parents that combing regularly with a fine-toothed comb could help them to both find and prevent head-lice.

A routine check-up became a learning experience which the children enjoyed immensely. They were fascinated by the enlarged pictures of head-lice – it was rather like enjoying a scary film.

Key vocabulary

clean, **dirty**, **wash**, **scrub**, **brush**, **teeth**, **hands**, **nails**, **toothpaste**, **soap**, **towel**, **water**, **nail-brush**, **handkerchief**, **tissue**, **germs**

Activities

You will need:

about 20–30 sheets of A5 card; a sheet of A1 card; pictures of a toothbrush, toothpaste, nail-brush, soap, flannel, towel, wash-basin, shower, bath, running tap and tissues; a role-play area set up as a bathroom; drawing and writing materials; scissors; glue; 'happy face' and 'sad face' stickers.

Preliminary discussions

● Ask the children when it is important to wash their hands. Their answers should include: before eating; after using the toilet; if they cut themselves; and after handling animals, plants or soil. The children might think of other times, such as after painting, making models, handling charcoal or using pastel crayons, when their hands get dirty enough for them to *see* the dirt.

● Ask the children what might be on their hands which they *can't* see. Do they know what germs can do? Talk about how germs can get into their bodies through their mouths and through cuts. Explain how they can stop this by washing their hands, washing and covering cuts and by making sure they do not put anything in their mouths which might have germs on it. Can they think of any examples of the last one?

After discussion

● Glue on to A5 card pictures of items which the children should use to keep themselves clean. They can take turns to pick up a card, name the item on it and say when and how they use it.

● Invite the children to use the picture cards to play a game in pairs. One child should choose a picture but not tell their partner which one it is. They should mime how it is used while their partner tries to work out which picture it is.

● Make a set of cards showing examples of good and bad hygiene, using invented characters (for example 'Mr Sparkle brushes his teeth every morning'; 'Miss Clean washes her hands before lunch'; 'Miss Sniff wipes her nose on her sleeve'; 'Mr and Mrs Mean share a toothbrush'). Read a card to the children and ask them to put a 'happy face' or 'sad face' sticker on it to show whether it represents 'good hygiene' or 'bad hygiene'. Display the cards and stickers, which the children could sort into two sets. The children could make up other cards to add to each set.

The children mimed the use of 'washing' items on picture cards for a partner to guess.

Assessment

● Can the children say when it is important to wash their hands, and why?

● Can they name activities which make their hands dirty?

● Do they wash their hands after using the toilet?

● Do they wash their hands after handling animals, plants or soil?

● Can they identify times when it is important to brush their teeth?

● Can they identify 'good' and 'bad' hygiene habits?

Evidence of the children's learning

The children added pictures to the 'good hygiene' and 'bad hygiene' display, including 'Mr Squeaky-Clean washes his hands before lunch', 'Miss Sneeze uses a tissue' and 'Miss Dirty never has a bath'.

In the role-play 'bathroom', one child took the role of the mother of a little girl who would not wash her hands. 'There will be millions of germs in your nails,' she said. 'You'll know when you're sick. You can have some sweets if you wash them...' adding, as an afterthought, '...if you promise to brush your teeth.'

Differentiating the activities

Provide dolls in a 'bathroom' equipped with towels, a flannel, a nail-brush, toothpaste, a toothbrush (warn the children not to put it in their mouths), soap, shampoo, etc. Display cut-out and labelled pictures of these items in the role-play area. The children can wash the dolls, scrub their nails, brush their teeth and so on.

Extension activities

With help, some children might be able to make a board game about keeping clean. The board can be a sheet of A1 card on to which sixteen A5 sheets of card can be glued. On each A5 card a child draws a 'good hygiene' or 'bad hygiene' picture. Draw arrows on the board to show the direction of play. You will also need about 20 'happy face' stickers on small pieces of card. The children take turns to throw a die and to move the appropriate number of squares. If they land on a 'good hygiene' square, they take a 'happy face' card. The winner is the player with the most cards when everyone has reached the end.

Involving parents

Help the children to make a 'check-up' card for one 'good hygiene' activity, such as brushing their teeth, washing their hands before a meal or using a handkerchief. Divide the card into sections, each representing a day of the week. Parents could put a tick in the box for each day on which the child carries out the 'good hygiene' action without being reminded.

Are the children allowed to have a bath alone? Ask them to describe, step by step, what they do. They could present this as 'instructions for having a bath' and could include the things they play with and the things for pouring water over themselves. Do they spend more time playing or washing? The children could contribute to a collage entitled 'Bath-time' which shows all the 'hygiene' items like soap, a flannel, bubble bath and a towel, and all the toys which are part of bath-time.

Is It Time? by Marilyn Janovitz
(North-South Books, 1996)

A wolf-cub is getting ready for bed. He knows his bed-time routine, and asks his mother if it is time for running the bath, brushing his teeth, dressing for bed, etc. The story is written as a rhyme so the children can join in once they know it.

After reading each double-page spread of the story, ask the children to predict what the little wolf-cub will do next and give them the opportunity to predict the rhyming words of each verse, for example:

> *Yes, it's time to run the tub.*
> *Is it time to rub-a-dub-???* [dub]
> and
> *Yes, it's time to use the towel.*
> *Is it time to give a ???* [howl]

Using stories and rhymes

Andrew's Bath by David McPhail
(Picture Puffins, 1988)

Andrew's bath is never quite right: it is too hot, too cold, too shallow or too deep; his mother scrubs him too hard or his father puts too much shampoo on his hair. Finally, Andrew's parents decide that he can have a bath by himself. The bath is perfect: the water is neither too hot nor too cold, nor too deep nor too shallow – and it is full of toys!

The children could talk about their night-time and morning routines for keeping clean. What do they do which is the same as the wolf-cub? What do they do which is different? Two spare copies of the book could be cut up to make picture cards which the children could sequence to show the correct order of the wolf-cub's night-time routine. They could draw and sequence pictures of their own bed-time routine, or make their own cards using pictures cut from magazines and catalogues.

Getting dressed

Intended learning

To encourage independence in dressing; to develop awareness of the clothing which is appropriate for different occasions.

Snapshot

Anyone who works with children up to the age of five will be aware of the many opportunities for children to practise putting on clothes and shoes (and just how long it can take!).

James was very good at putting on, taking off and fastening aprons, shoes and coats. He could put on his jumper the right way around and get his shoes on to the correct feet. He was also very good at helping his friend Sasha, who could not manage so well, and enjoyed showing off his skills. Sasha made no attempt to do these things for herself because she had such a willing helper. There were other children in the nursery, like Sasha, who always seemed to be able to find someone to fasten buttons, tie shoe-laces and zip up their coats for them. Mrs Dhanjal decided to ask the children who could do these things to *show* the others, rather than do it for them. Each child who learned a new skill was applauded by the rest of the class during one of the Friday end-of-day discussions.

Mrs Dhanjal recognised that children can learn some skills from one another just as well as, and sometimes better than, from the teacher. In asking some children to teach the others, she recognised and praised their skills and helped to develop their self-esteem. Those who learned each new skill were given public recognition. Mrs Dhanjal also avoided spending her own time teaching button-fastening, lace-tying and so on.

Key vocabulary

warm, **hot**, **cold**, **cool**, **wet**, **dry**, **fasten**, **tie**, **buckle**, **button**, **zip**, **Velcro**

Activities

You will need:

Shoes with different kinds of fasteners; zip-up jackets; Velcro-fastening aprons, shoes and jackets; button-up cardigans, shirts and jackets; coats with toggles; diplay dummies borrowed from a shop; a range of clothing for dressing the dummy; drawing materials; scissors; magazines and catalogues; a computer.

Preliminary discussions

● Talk about the clothes which the children are wearing. They could demonstrate how to put on (and fasten, where appropriate) various clothes, such as a pullover, a shirt, a jacket with toggles or buttons, a zip-up jacket and shoes with laces or buckles.

● How did the children decide what to wear today? Did their parents tell them what to wear? Do they wear the same clothes at home? If not, can they explain why not?

● Ask the children to name the type of shoes they are wearing. When do they change their shoes and why? (They might wear slippers indoors when they are at home, training shoes for sports, wellingtons when it rains and so on.)

After discussion

● A wall display could be made of everyday clothes worn by the children. The children could help to label the display, and help the rest of the class to read the labels they have made.

● Provide male and female shop dummies for the children to dress for a particular activity or occasion. The children could choose from three or four instruction cards which could include a picture of the setting for the activity, or occasion, for example: 'Dress Fred for playing football' or 'Dress Freda for her wedding'. Include among the clothing and equipment such things as: nurse and police uniforms; a cycling safety helmet; a jacket, belt or band which shows up easily in the dark; a football kit; tennis clothes; roller-blading safety items, such as knee and elbow pads; a cricket kit; an angler's wet-weather outfit; and a horse-riding kit.

● The children could cut out pictures of people from magazines or catalogues and glue them on to a background depicting a location for which they are dressed, such as a beach, a swimming pool, a room containing a wedding cake on a table, a football or cricket pitch, a playground, bicycles or a gym.

● Provide a computer (and software) which allows the children to use the mouse to drag and drop clothing on to a picture of a child (or on to a teddy bear, as in *Dress Teddy* in *My World*, for the Acorn computer).

The children enjoyed looking through catalogues to find pictures of children dressed for the playground.

Assessment

● Can the children match pictures of people, by what they are wearing, to pictures of occasions or activities?

● Can they identify clothes which people wear for specific types of work?

● Can they select clothing to wear in different weather conditions?

● Can they put on and take off clothing such as a coat, an apron and shoes?

● Can they fasten buttons and a zip?

● Can they tie shoe-laces?

Evidence of the children's learning

One child told a teddy bear to wear his sun-hat 'or you'll get a sun-stroke'. She dressed him in shorts, a T-shirt, sunglasses and a baseball cap.

Children using the computer program *Dress Teddy* sometimes got the clothes in the wrong order: for example, putting on Teddy's shoes and then realising that he did not have his socks on. They soon learned to remove Teddy's shoes by dragging and dropping them with the mouse, to put on his socks, and then to collect his shoes and put them back on him. They could answer questions such as 'Which does Teddy put on first, his shoes or his socks?' and 'Which does he put on first, his hat or his coat?', and to say whether or not the order mattered.

Differentiating the activities

Provide teddy bears and dolls, and clothes which will fit them, including a coat, a hat, a jumper, a dress, a skirt, shorts, a T-shirt, socks, shoes and underwear. After the children have dressed a doll or teddy bear, can they remember in which order they put on the clothes? They could arrange the clothes in a line in the order in which they think they put them on. Ask them to check that the order is correct, by dressing the doll again. They could draw the clothes in the correct order, then help them to label each item of clothing.

Extension activities

● Make 'practice' displays by fixing a real item of clothing with fasteners on to a display board. Include clothes with buttons, laces, Velcro, toggles, zip fasteners and buckles. Include a chart showing the children's names and the different types of fastener in the display. The children cut put a 'happy face' sticker on the chart when they can do up a fastener.

● Provide the children with an outline of a child. Let them add features and hair, and then use the outline as a template for drawing clothes, which they can colour and cut from paper. Ask them to dress the figure for an occasion (such as a wedding), for work, for sport, or for different weather conditions (such as hot weather, rain or snow).

● The children could draw pictures of themselves in the summer and in the winter, to show the different clothing they wear. Help them to label the clothes.

Involving parents

Parents could encourage the children to dress themselves. Provide each child with a small card on which they can draw pictures of the things they wear for school. When they can dress themselves with a garment, they and their parents can put a tick against the picture.

Using stories and rhymes

Buster Keeps Warm by Rod Campbell (Campbell Books, 1988)

Buster gets dressed for a cold day, starting with his underwear, socks and a T-shirt. The pages are split so that the children can always see the words of one page ('Buster puts on his'...). As they turn the pages, they can see the pictures and read the words which tell them what he puts on in the correct order: a woolly hat, trousers, a jumper, boots, a coat, a scarf and gloves.

After reading the book, ask the children to take turns to name the clothes which Buster put on, in the order he put them on. Could he have put them on in a different order? They could draw and cut out pictures of Buster's clothes and arrange them in different, but correct, orders. Ask them questions which include the words 'before' or 'after', such as: 'Could Buster put on his coat *before* his T-shirt?' and 'Could he put on his jumper *after* his boots?'. The children could make their own books with split pages to show Buster dressing for a cold day or a hot day.

Cleversticks by Bernard Ashley (HarperCollins, 1992)

Ling Sung cannot tie his shoe-laces: 'his fingers get tangled up and the laces keep going their own ways'. He watches while Terry ties and unties his over and over again, while everyone in the nursery watches and claps. Anis can fasten the Velcro tabs on an apron, but Ling Sung cannot. He is fed up with clapping other people for the things they can do. Then he eats a broken biscuit, chop-stick style, using paint brushes – everyone claps him and the teachers ask him to show the others how he did it. Then the others help him with his apron, his shoes and his buttons.

Invite those children who can, to demonstrate how to put on and fasten everyday clothes. Ask them what was the secret way in which Sharon told Ling Sung to fasten buttons so that he would not get them wrong. ('Start at the top and go down, or at the bottom and go up. Don't start in the middle.') Help the children to do up other fastenings by giving them similar, simple instructions. Their parents might have other useful tips which could be passed on.

Resources

What Do I Look Like? Nick Sharratt 1998 (Walker)

The Magical Bicycle Berlie Doherty 1996 (Collins Picture Lions)

I Can Build a House Shigeo Watanabe 1982 (Red Fox)

I Feel Sad Brian Moses 1994 (Wayland)

What I Like Catherine & Laurence Anholt 1998 (Walker)

Waiting for my Shorts to Dry Michelle Margorian 1989 (Picture Puffins)

The Big Book of Families Catherine & Laurence Anholt 1998 (Walker)

Something Special Nicola Moon 1995 (Orchard)

Bye Bye Baby Janet & Allan Ahlberg 1991 (Mammoth)

The Mice Who Lived in a Shoe Rodney Peppé 1981 (Picture Puffins)

Little Bean's Friend John Wallace 1996 (Collins Picture Lions)

Chatting Shirley Hughes 1994 (Walker)

Handa's Surprise Eileen Brown 1994 (Walker)

The Bad-Tempered Ladybird Eric Carle 1977 (Picture Puffins)

This is Our House Michael Rosen 1996 (Walker)

Giving Shirley Hughes 1995 (Walker)

The Oxford Nursery Rhyme Book Iona & Peter Opie 1997 (Oxford University Press)

The House that Jack Built Traditional 1987 (Ladybird)

Goodnight Owl Pat Hutchins 1972 (Picture Puffins)

This is the Bear Sarah Hayes 1986 (Walker)

Little Miss Tidy Roger Hargreaves 1990 (World International)

I Don't Care Brian Moses & Mike Gordon 1997 (Wayland)

The Tiny Seed Eric Carle 1997 (Picture Puffins)

Kipper's Birthday Mick Inkpen 1993 (Hodder & Stoughton)

When Frank Was Four Alison Lester 1997 (Little Ark, Allen & Unwin)

Getting Ready for Eid Roderick Hunt 1994 (Oxford University Press)

The Oxford Nursery Book Ian Beck 1995 (Oxford University Press)

Bedtime Bears Susanna Gretz 1990 (Hippo/Scholastic)

Avocado Baby John Burningham 1994 (Red Fox)

The Baked Bean Queen Rose Impey & Sue Porter 1986 (Picture Puffins)

Andrew's Bath David McPhail 1988 (Picture Puffins)

Is It Time? Marilyn Janovitz 1996 (North-South Books)

Buster Keeps Warm Rod Campbell 1988 (Campbell Books)

My World Acorn Software

Cleversticks Bernard Ashley 1992 (HarperCollins)

First published 1999 by A & C Black (Publishers) Ltd, 35 Bedford Row, London WC1R 4JH

Text copyright © Christine Moorcroft 1999. Illustrations copyright © Alison Dexter 1999.

Classroom photographs copyright © Zul Mukhida 1999; Studio photographs copyright © Ken Travis 1999

ISBN 0-7136-4926-7

A CIP catalogue record for this book is available from the British Library.

Printed in Hong Kong through Colorcraft Ltd.